The Smoking Hills

Also by Carter Travis Young

The Smoking Hills

CARTER TRAVIS YOUNG

DOUBLEDAY & COMPANY, INC.

GARDEN CITY, NEW YORK

1988

Library of Congress Cataloging-in-Publication Data

Young, Carter Travis.
The smoking hills.

I. Title.
PS3575.07S6   1988   813'.54   86-29060
ISBN: 0-385-24059-7

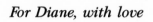

For Diane, with love

The Smoking Hills

1

Cullom Blaine was riding slowly across a rolling highland between two arms of the Guadalupe range when he came on the pony tracks. Three ponies, all of them unshod.

He pulled up and sat a little hipshot in the saddle, staring down. It was midmorning and he could feel the sun hot on his back. He eased his battered Stetson back on his head with a knuckle.

These were the third set of Indian pony tracks he had seen in the last twenty-four hours. Each time there were three or four riders in a group, and all moved in the same direction. The direction from which the smoke curled above the hills.

The tracks and the talking smoke confirmed what Blaine had heard from a surly prospector he had happened upon two days before. The prospector had been coming down one of the canyons along the eastern flank of these mountains. He had been heading for civilization with his scalp and his news.

Navaja was loose. In these rugged mountains, where the cavalry would have one hell of a time digging him out.

It was not the first time the young Apache renegade known as Navaja—the Knife—had broken out of the reservation. And this time, as before, he would have had little trouble persuading a band of young hotheads to follow him in defiance of the hated peace treaty. Last winter, Blaine had heard, after Navaja's brother had been killed in one of a series of running skirmishes with the army, the renegade had led the remnants of his starving band back to the dubious succor of the Indian reservation. The army had not whipped him; winter had. So men said. The long hard winter had starved Navaja into doing something that must have eaten at him ever since, like a worm inside an apple. So they said.

But this was another summer, and Blaine wondered if a proud maverick like Navaja would come in again. If that pride would let him come in again while he was alive.

Squinting in the midday glare, Blaine peered over his shoulder along his own trail. The Indian pony tracks led southeast, the direction from which he had come. Scanning the bright hard sky he saw no curls or puffs of smoke, but they had been there earlier. He was not fooled by the fact that he had seen no one. They had seen *him.* And let him pass.

Why?

He thought of the stagecoach station he had skirted the evening before, passing close enough to see the light from a window of the station, close enough to smell the smoke from a cooking fire. Blaine had had no wish to have his passage noted. Like Navaja, he was a hunted renegade.

But the Apache wasn't running. He was heading *toward* Cheever's Station. He wasn't acting the way he should have, and that brought a thoughtful speculation to Blaine's eyes, which seemed as bright as jewels in his hard, sun-dark face.

Blaine was aware of being in the open, skylined on the top of the high meadow. But it was motion that caught the eye, and both man and horse were so dusty and weathered that, motionless, they were almost invisible, one with the land.

After a moment Blaine nudged his horse toward the

nearest draw. They dropped off the table into a deep canyon, following a well-worn trail that overlooked the spill of a stream cutting its way down to the canyon floor. There Blaine dismounted, watered the buckskin briefly, and turned the horse onto a patch of grass near a bend in the stream. After filling his canteen, Blaine dug some jerked beef out of his pack. Chewing helped a man think.

Blaine sat with his back propped against a scrub oak that seemed to be growing out of solid rock. He stared at the play of light where the stream darted over its shallow bed.

There was a pool a short distance below him, and a large speckled trout hovered just beneath the surface of the pool. Blaine flicked a pebble at him and the trout vanished.

The canyon was surprisingly verdant. There were walnut and ash and maple trees as well as oaks. Back up the canyon there was also pine and fir. Below there was thick grass and a profusion of yellow flowers.

Cheever's Station was near the mouth of another of these canyons. The overland trail from St. Louis had created the station as a stop on the stage route to California. At the time Blaine passed by there had been little activity, though he had seen a half-dozen horses in the corral and smoke from the chimney of the stone-walled station. No doubt there were a few travelers, up from Fort Tracy to the south, waiting for the next stage.

What was Navaja after? Why wasn't he running north, losing himself in the wilderness of the mountain range that thrust deep into New Mexico, or south into Mexico, long a favorite hideout for the Mescalero Apaches?

Restless over the direction his thoughts were taking, Blaine tossed another pebble and watched the ripples spread across the quiet surface of the pool.

For him the Apaches might be a blessing in disguise. There were enough men dogging his trail to stumble over each other, like a pack of overexcited hounds closing in on their prey. Having Navaja and his outlaws come between Blaine and his pursuers could only work to his advantage. The Clancy brothers, fresh out of Huntsville Penitentiary, would not take chances with their scalps. Life would be too precious to them after prison. Marshal J. P. Holifield was not far behind, nursing his own hatred, and Navaja's presence would divert or delay him. As for others on his trail, Blaine had only rumors to rely on, pricklings of warning. It was whispered that the Clancy brothers had set a price on Cullom Blaine's head. That could mean hunters eager to find him for reasons other than the hatred and fear that pushed the Clancy brothers and the marshal. Greed was an emotion almost as powerful, but an Apache wolf pack might make any bounty hunter cautious.

Like a man who has already made up his mind but seeks out reasons to buttress his decision, Blaine let the arguments play out. Navaja was unpredictable, but the isolated way station was a vulnerable target. The Indians might need horses, food, guns. Navaja might simply want scalps to whet the blood thirst of his braves. Certainly he would relish some sort of victory to salve the bitter memory of last winter's defeat.

But it wasn't Cullom Blaine's problem. He owed nothing to the strangers at Cheever's Station. If he went back —even to warn them—he risked being caught with them in the same trap if Navaja chose to spring it. And if he escaped that trap, he might well blunder into another, set by one of the hunters.

Cullom Blaine did not want a showdown with Marshal J. P. Holifield. He hadn't wanted it the first time they met

—Holifield had forced it on him. Backtracking to Cheever's Station almost certainly meant letting Holifield get close enough to pick up the scent once more. A fool's choice. Only a fool volunteered to help knot the rope that would be used to hang him.

The Clancy brothers were another matter. Blaine *wanted* them to come after him.

Blaine swallowed the last chaw of tough dried beef, washing it down with clear, cool water from the stream. He caught up the buckskin's reins and rode back up the canyon toward the highland trail he had been following.

Let Navaja do what he would. Blaine would gain needed time if his pursuers were delayed because of the Apache. Time to lose himself in the mountains to the northwest. Time to set his own trap.

He had reached the open meadow and turned west when he heard the first thin rifle shot, echoing among the rocky canyons like a far-off trumpet call. By the time the second shot came Blaine had already swung around and kneed the buckskin into a run.

2

In his despair Noah Calder gazed across the empty plain as if he were staring into hell itself. It was certainly hot enough, he thought with bleak humor. There was a blazing light over the land, harsher and yet also clearer, brighter than any he had known back in Ohio, so that everything stood out in purer forms and colors, the pink of the rugged bluffs, white rocks, crisp black shadows, vivid dark green of pines marching down the flank of the higher hills to the north. Only the scrub brush on the desert floor seemed to have had most of its color leached away.

The little jump seat wagon in which Noah rode with his young bride, Charity, moved at a desultory pace, pulled by the sturdy bay horse given to them when they were banished from the Ohio community. "She will pull well," Noah's father had told him grimly, thin mouth pulled into a tight, unforgiving line, on the morning Noah and Charity had left the village. The horse, along with $100 and a sack of flour, were gifts awarded the young couple, according to Shaker custom, when they were sent away after violating the prohibition against any form of commingling between a man and a woman.

Now the bay was tiring. So, Noah knew, was Charity, though she would not complain. Beneath the bonnet that shadowed her face her features were drawn, her lips cracked and sore, burned dry by the merciless heat. And yet, Noah thought with a fullness of heart, with her lips cracked and her eyes dark with fatigue and her clothes caked with dust, she was as pretty as a spring morning fresh with dew.

They were alone, lost, and after nearly two days of wandering in growing desperation Noah Calder was confronting the possibility that they might never stumble upon the trail of the wagons which had left them behind, or even upon another track that might lead them to some settlement or human habitation of any kind.

The problem had surfaced the previous morning when the small wagon train broke camp at dawn. Hurriedly preparing to leave with the others, in the midst of the usual morning confusion, Noah had discovered to his dismay that the right rear wheel of the light wagon on which they had traveled from St. Louis was loose, a linchpin sheared off. And Noah had already used his last replacement pin.

Noah had known there would be trouble as soon as he saw the sullen resistance in Joseph Haller's face. Haller was the leader of the small group of pilgrims, and he had taken an unaccountable dislike to the young couple in the jump seat wagon. Noah expected the attitude had something to do with religious disapproval. Their dress set them apart, to begin with, the plain dress common to all Shaker communities. Noah wondered if, now that they were of the world's people, he and Charity should dress like them, but he had hesitated to suggest it. Haller's attitude seemed to have communicated itself to the other wagon families, and the Calders had found themselves isolated from the normal friendly activity of the night camps. Now, moreover, he was told that no one had any spare linchpins. He knew the statement to be untrue but could not call Haller a liar.

"I'll have it fixed in an hour," Noah had assured Haller, who regarded him with hostile skepticism.

"We can't hold up the whole train. We're already behind schedule."

"An hour can't make that much difference."

"We have only your notion you'll have your wagon fixed in an hour."

Noah knew that the lost time was not the real reason for Haller's reluctance. The members of the train had become increasingly apprehensive during the last few days, especially since the morning when a plume of smoke over the distant hills had been excitedly identified as Indian smoke signals. Rumors flew about the camp of Indian troubles, of other trains struck suddenly by bloodthirsty savages. There were eight wagons of an original group of twelve. One had dropped out early when a wagon broke down. Others had not been ready to leave in time—or had been afraid. The decision to set off with the smaller group, many now felt, had been dangerously foolhardy.

And why should they wait, risking their necks, for this young Shaker couple whom they had already decided to shun?

"You'll have to catch up," Joseph Haller said stubbornly, not meeting Noah's eyes as he made the pronouncement. "If you've got the wheel fixed in an hour as you say, you'll have no trouble catching up."

Pride made Noah swallow his angry protest.

Halfway through that morning he cursed his youthful pride. He had trouble finding anything in his gear to use as a replacement for the broken pin. He tried making a wooden one, whittled down from a green branch. By the time he had it thin enough to fit, it was no longer strong enough to hold. The wheel came off before they had traveled a hundred feet.

It was past noon, the sun hot overhead in a brassy sky, when they finally set off in pursuit of the vanished wagon train. The right rear wheel of the wagon was a little wobbly but held in place, secured to the axle by a pin Noah had made from the handle of one of Charity's iron cooking pots.

Through the afternoon there was no sign of the other wagons, not even a plume of dust, though the trail was clear enough to follow. Then the trail took an abrupt turn south. Noah saw that the train was attempting to detour around some rugged bluffs. Eventually they would have to swing west once more, and they would have lost considerable time circling to the south before coming back to their true course. But Noah had also spotted a narrow trail that led due west into a canyon. It was a well-beaten track, and Noah was certain that there were wagon ruts among the tracks of animals and others who had made this path through the hills. He reasoned that the trail would not be so well worn unless it led through the hills. Nervous about the prospect of spending the night alone with Charity in the middle of this vast wilderness, Noah chose to gamble on shortening the distance between them and the other wagons. With luck they would catch up before dark.

Luck did not ride with them. Dusk found the gates of the canyon drawing shut, the walls closing in, the well-worn trail petering out as the canyon bottom narrowed to a tumble of rocks.

Noah turned back. He had led them into a blind canyon.

They spent the night near the mouth of the canyon, shivering with cold and fright, listening to the eerie howls of animals—wolves or coyotes—from the high darkness of the hills.

In the morning they set off again, trying to keep to the

trail of the wagons ahead of them, but even this sign, earlier so plain, all but disappeared after a brief squall swept down from the western hills, a half hour of rolling thunder, lightning and a hard-driving rain. The storm swept eastward and the sun was soon out, seemingly hotter than before, steam rising from the prairie. But an hour later the land was once again as dry as the bones that littered the desert floor, only an occasional small pool of water captured in the cup of a rock showing that there had been any rain at all.

Noah kept the sun at their backs through the morning of this second day on their own. He followed it into the afternoon as it began to drop toward the western horizon. By then he knew that they were lost. They could only keep on, moving always westward. But for how long?

The vastness of the land overwhelmed him. Its sheer size diminished a man, while at the same time kindling a kind of awe. Who could doubt God in such a place? And who would not call out to Him for relief from his despair?

"Oh, my heavens!" Charity cried.

Noah glanced at her quickly, for she was not given to such exclamations. Then he followed her gaze toward the bluffs on their right. There, on the line of a ridge shimmering in the heat haze, so dark against the blue brightness of the sky that they were like cutout silhouettes, were three men on horseback.

Not just men. Indians!

At the first wild tug of alarm Noah's hands instinctively reined in the bay. Then the same panicky instinct urged him to lash the horse into a run. But he hesitated, unsure, his heart hammering, throat dry. Where could they run? There was no place in all this vast emptiness to hide.

And they were helpless to defend themselves. Noah owned no weapon. Violence was against his creed.

"Who . . . who are they, Noah?"

"Indians," he said. "Savages."

Charity did not reply. She continued to stare at the small black figures on the rim, one hand at her throat. Sunlight glinted off metal. A lance? A rifle carried by one of the savages?

"We will try to make a run. The other wagons may not be so far ahead as we think." Noah Calder spoke in a low, unsteady voice, wishing that he could keep the fear out of it. "Charity . . ."

"What is it, Noah?"

"I am sorry I got thee into this fix," he said. It was the nearest he had ever come to expressing regret over the decision—and its harsh repercussions—which had brought them to this lonely place, far from home and friends and all they had known in their short lives.

"It was not thy doing, Noah," she said quietly.

"Well, if it wasn't my doing, I'd like to know—" He broke off.

"It was mine," she said simply. "I'd made up my mind to it, that's all."

Noah Calder could feel his neck and ears reddening, hot under the wide flat brim of his black hat. The implications were too much to take in out of the blue like this.

Then the Indians vanished from the rim as if they had never been there, like a mirage disappearing, and in his startled reaction Noah cracked the reins and shouted "Hah!" at the bay and the horse leaped forward, jerking the wagon behind her. Charity grabbed the iron railing at the edge of the padded bench seat with one hand, her bonnet with the other.

The little wagon bounced and rocked over the uneven ground. Dust boiled around them, enveloping the wagon and its two occupants, spilling out behind them. Noah quickly brought the bay under control but let her run, his glance flicking toward the naked bluffs to the right where the Indians had been.

They pounded around a huge outcropping of pink rock and his heart leaped. The Indians were racing on their ponies down a long flank of the hills, their course on a line to intercept the wagon.

Wildly Noah looked around. The way ahead was open but would bring them directly into the path of the savages. The bluffs blocked any turn to the north, and on the left the land was a wasteland of scrub brush and shallow ravines and rock spills. The right rear wheel had been damaged earlier trying to ride over such terrain.

He hauled back on the reins and pulled the bay around. There was no way out. Nothing to do but turn about and run.

In his turmoil Charity's words came back to him. "It was not thy doing, Noah. It was mine." How could that be? Her words meant that she had desired him as much as he had wanted her—that the self-loathing and recriminations he had inflicted on himself across two thousand miles were not entirely his burden. He had tongue-lashed himself a hundred times for ruining her life, tearing her from her own people through his selfishness, thrusting her unwilling into a future whose only certainties were danger and deprivation. Now that was being turned upside down . . .

"Noah!"

Charity's cry cut through his wild thoughts. In the same instant he heard the crack of a rifle.

3

From the top of the bluffs Cullom Blaine gazed down on the bizarre scene several hundred yards away on the valley floor. The small wagon was of a type familiar back East, resembling a buggy with a fixed top, the two rear wheels larger than those on the front. Its canopy was rigid and flat, suspended over a small flatbed behind a single bench seat. The wagon was light enough to be pulled by one horse in shafts, this one a bay which reared up in panic as Blaine watched. The driver fought to keep the horse under control.

Around the wagon a trio of Apaches circled, firing their rifles into the air or at the feet of the bay. Yips and yelps of laughter carried clearly to the top of the bluff. The Indians were engaged in a cruel game, taunting and tormenting the helpless couple in the little wagon.

Two people. A man and a woman, dressed in black or dark clothing of some kind. Easterners, by the look of them and their wagon. Tenderfoot pilgrims. What had brought them to this desolate valley alone?

And why hadn't they defended themselves?

Ironically that failure had—so far—saved their lives, allowing the Apaches to indulge in sport at their expense. Resistance would have brought swift and brutal reprisal.

But the Apaches would soon tire of their sport. What would happen next was not hard to envisage. The cruelty of the Apache toward his enemies was legendary, a bottomless well, as much a part of his nature as cunning and bravery in battle.

They had not seen Blaine watching from the rim above them. The sun was behind him and in their eyes. He looked down from between two humps of rock, so that he presented no clear outline, and he was also partially screened by the upper branches of a gnarled manzanita tree that grew mysteriously out of what seemed to be solid rock in the face of the limestone bluff.

Blaine wormed away from the edge on his belly until he was out of sight of the Apaches before he stood. His rangy buckskin waited where Blaine had tied him to a stunted cedar. Blaine drew his rifle from its boot. It was a Winchester center-fire repeating rifle, and its .44-40 cartridge had an advantage Blaine particularly liked. He had to buy only one kind of shell, for the big old Walker Colt six-shooter he carried on his hip was chambered to handle the same size cartridge as the Winchester. The rifle had a twenty-four-inch barrel and a fifteen-shot magazine, and using it Blaine had felled deer with a single shot at distances up to five hundred yards.

The Apaches were not that far away. Blaine was fairly sure that he could drop all three before they could reach cover. Their sport had lured them out onto the floor of the valley with no real cover within fifty yards of them, neither rock nor tree. Not that an Apache needed much more than a little patch of grass to lose himself.

Back at the rim Blaine studied the Indians circling the wagon. One of the Apaches was evidently their leader. He stood out from the others as much from his bearing as his size, though he was broad through back and shoulders, and taller than most Apaches. Unlike his two followers, who wore ragged shirts, he was naked above the waist, wearing only breechclout and leggings. He rode a handsome, muscular pony, brown and white with a black mane, his fingers digging into the mane and making the pony one with him, so that horse and rider seemed to move as a single force. That pony would mean a lot to the rider, Blaine thought. Almost as much as his own life.

Blaine sighted on the brown-and-white pony, then waited for the second rider's dun-colored horse to dance into his sights before he squeezed the trigger.

The *whack!* of the rifle shot bounced off the surrounding bluffs and rattled in the deep canyons. The dun bucked in panic, throwing its rider. The Apache rolled as he landed, quickly scurrying to his feet, his gaze on the bluffs, searching. Blaine squeezed off four more shots in rapid sequence, spacing them deliberately in a track at the feet of the dun and leading toward the leader's handsome pony.

The message was clear. Blaine had given the leader of the Apaches a choice. Run, leaving his hapless victims in their wagon unharmed, or lose his pony.

The choice offered was also an honorable one. The message also said that the Apaches themselves could easily have been the targets of the first round of fire.

The leader wheeled his brown-and-white pony. He threw one challenging glance toward the top of the limestone cliff before gesturing to the other Indians, pointing to the south. The unhorsed Apache ran toward the dun, which had calmed down, vaulted onto its back, and raced off down the valley behind the leader.

Blaine watched them across the long bottom until they disappeared. Then he rode along the top of the bluffs parallel to the Indians' trail for several minutes, following the line of their dust.

The Apaches could have sent one rider on ahead as a decoy while the others doubled back. Blaine doubted it.

They could not be certain how many enemies watched from the high bluffs. And the young pilgrims in the wagon, who did not even fight back, were not of much interest to them. Not worth losing a fine pony for.

Blaine rode down a long slope to the valley floor and swung back toward the little wagon. The young man had climbed down from the bench seat and watched Blaine as he rode toward them. The woman remained where she was.

Blaine drew in and sat relaxed in the saddle, slouched a little to one side, regarding the young pilgrims. Hardly twenty years of age, he judged, the woman even younger. The man wore a long, square-skirted, bluish gray coat, plain gray trousers, and a very wide-brimmed black hat that dwarfed his lean features. He had close-cropped black hair and gray eyes that were alert and questioning above a long thin nose. The young woman wore a long dress of gray homespun cloth with a white three-cornered kerchief over her shoulders and bosom and a starched white bonnet, from which a few blond curls had strayed. Their clothing seemed absurdly inappropriate for the hot dry desert through which they were journeying in their little wagon. Blaine could see a small cargo of belongings in the bed of the wagon behind the bench seat.

"Were thee the one who fired on those savages from above?" the young man asked. "If so, I thank thee, friend."

Blaine said, "You are unarmed." It was not a question.

"It is against our beliefs," the young man said, a little defensively, Blaine thought. It was hard to sit still while someone made sport of you, whatever your convictions.

"You are Quakers, then?" Blaine had known many members of the Society of Friends in the small Pennsylvania town where he had grown up, west of Lancaster.

"No, sir, though we hold to many of the same beliefs about the usage of arms against another. We are known as Shakers. That is . . ." He hesitated before adding, "We were such, until we were sent away."

"We do not believe in violence," the young woman said, breaking her silence.

"Apaches do," Blaine said.

"Would the . . . the Indians have killed us if thee had not intervened?"

"It's likely," Blaine said curtly. "When they were done with you."

She did not flinch. Young as she was, she had recovered her composure remarkably quickly, Blaine thought. And beneath the plain dress and starched bonnet was a pretty face, the blue eyes large and steady, lips neither prim nor pouting.

"Then we are doubly grateful, are we not, Mr. Calder?"

"Yes, indeed. Oh . . . I am Noah Calder, friend, and this is my wife, Charity. We were separated from our wagon train, and it seems we are lost. I don't suppose thee could direct us toward the nearest settlement . . . ?"

Blaine was silent a moment, thinking of the deceptive ease with which the Apaches had been induced to abandon their sport. "There's a stagecoach station not far," he said at length. "You would have come to it if the Apaches hadn't decided to have fun with you."

The reminder sobered young Calder. "Does thee think they will return, Mr. . . . ?"

"I doubt it," Blaine said. He did not offer his name, though it would mean nothing to the pilgrims. "But you can never tell with Apaches. Anyway, if you sit here waiting, someone else you don't want to meet is sure to come along. I'm going that way myself, so you can follow along until we reach the station."

Noah and Charity Calder exchanged glances as he hast-
ily turned the wagon and set off in the strange rider's
wake. Charity took note of the fact that the rider moved
out to the right so that his horse's dust did not kick up into
the faces of the occupants of the wagon. Studying him
from the back, she saw a well-made man with wide, heavy
shoulders and a lean waist. He wore a wide-brimmed,
battered black hat and clothes that were well worn and
coated with dust. No way of telling how tall he was while
in the saddle, except that he was of good size. His eyes, set
above high cheekbones in his gaunt, weathered face,
were what she recalled most clearly. They had regarded
her with a sharp appraisal that offered nothing and asked
for no more.

She knew nothing of him except that he had intervened
to save them from the Indians. But in spite of his abrupt
manner she felt a total confidence in him. He had the
solidity of one of these limestone cliffs, she thought. More
than solidity. He was a man with no give in him, stubborn
and unyielding, as if, should he set himself in your way,
you would have to run right over him to get by. Or turn
aside.

"He did not give his name," she said after a while. "Who
do you suppose he is?"

"I don't know," Noah Calder said, "but he saved our
necks, and that is introduction enough for me!"

Riding on ahead, after reluctantly committing himself
to escorting the young pilgrims to Cheever's Station, Cullom Blaine's thoughts remained occupied with the
Apache on the brown-and-white pony. His command
over the others had been plain. There had been no hesitation, no quarreling or hanging back over the decision to
abandon their sport. No Apache liked to run. He lived to

fight and despised cowardice above all things. So the leader of the trio was someone to be reckoned with. Someone of importance.

Blaine had a hunch. All of the Indian tracks he had come across had been heading in this general direction. They were meant to come together, perhaps before this day's sun had set. The smoking hills had been a summons. The eager young braves who answered it would make a formidable band when they were joined, especially if the warrior who led them was one who commanded their loyalty and their passion.

A warrior like Navaja.

4

They approached the station at dusk, Blaine riding without haste but with every sense alive, knowing they were not alone, the little jump seat wagon close behind. They came in from the east, where there were only low hills and then a long open stretch so you could see the station from a mile off, see smoke curling up against a skyline rimmed blood-red. Rugged cliffs broken by deep canyons bulked to the north and more hills swelled to the south, though these were not as formidable, rounded off and less rocky, covered with clusters of cedar and scrub brush. Alert, for it was a dangerous time of day, the light deceptive, shadows undefined, Blaine watched not so much for shapes as for movement or a stirring of dust where there should be none. He saw nothing, heard nothing, but he knew they were there, the Apaches, and was certain that they knew they had little to fear from an attack in numbers against one armed man. The couple in the wagon, they knew, would offer no resistance.

Why hadn't they attacked?

When he came over the low rise east of the station and saw it in the distance Blaine understood. Fifteen or more mounted troopers were grouped before the station; others were leading their horses back to the group after watering them. Their attitudes were relaxed, and Blaine and the wagon had covered half the distance between them before he saw one of the troopers point toward them, and a uniformed man—an officer, he was certain—stepped from the dimness of the covered veranda and peered eastward.

The officer stepped down from the veranda and moved forward as the odd little group rode up to the station. The officer looked curiously from Blaine to the couple in the wagon. Blaine was aware of others on the veranda or emerging from the dim interior of the station. He saw a slim young woman and, next to her, recognized Art Cheever, a tall, stoop-shouldered man, balding on top of his head but with hair at the back and sides grown long, straggling over his neck and shoulders. Blaine knew little about him except that he owned the station—the story was that he had won it in a poker game—which operated as a stagecoach stop, general store and resting place. Cheever probably also did a little trading with the older, more peaceful Indians.

"Evening," the officer said. "Lieutenant Wilson, U.S. Cavalry. You've come from the east?"

"More north of here," Blaine said, "beyond those hills."

The officer glanced at the couple in the wagon with curiosity, taking in their dress and obvious fatigue. "You're traveling together?"

Blaine did not resent the cavalryman's curiosity. If he had come up from Fort Tracy to the south, he wanted to know that travelers had arrived safely from the east.

"Nay, friend, we were with a group of wagons," Noah Calder spoke up. He climbed down from the bench seat. "Have any been seen coming this way? I do not expect they were so far ahead of us."

"Some wagons come through midday," Art Cheever said from the veranda. "They didn't stop but for water and some flour." He seemed aggrieved that the wagons had offered little gain.

"That will be the others," Noah said to his wife, looking up at her anxiously.

"You encountered no trouble traveling?" Wilson asked.

"Nay!" Noah said quickly. "We were attacked by Indians, and it was this man who saved us."

Everyone turned to stare at Blaine, slouched in the saddle, a dusty figure who did not look like someone fresh from a scrape with warlike Comanches or Apaches. He was aware of quickened interest from the troopers nearby. "Is that true, sir?" the lieutenant asked sharply.

Blaine nodded. "Apaches are out there. Could be Navaja from what I hear. There were only three of them around these pilgrims when I come along, and they didn't seem to think it worth a fight. But I cut sign yesterday and today of others. I'd guess there's a dozen or more, and others on the way."

"Navaja!" Lieutenant Wilson exclaimed. "You're sure of that?"

"I didn't see him up close."

"I didn't think so." There was a faint smile on Wilson's lips. "We'd know it if that one had left the reservation." He glanced again at Noah and Charity Calder. "You say you were attacked? Traveling alone? I see no arrows or bullet holes." His smile had broadened.

"Nay, friend, but—"

"Then it was no Apache war party you ran into, for which you can be grateful. If you saw Indians in this territory they were most likely Comanches, not Apaches, and they are currently at peace with us."

"But they had surrounded us—they wouldn't let us by . . ."

"They were probably curious about you, sir, and your wife. You are not, after all, dressed in a manner familiar to the Indians, and I doubt they have seen a wagon quite like this one either."

Blaine studied the officer with rising irritation. He had the brisk self-assurance of the West Pointer new to command and a stranger to defeat. A muscular, vigorous man in his late twenties with sharp blue eyes and a flourishing blond mustache, he did not seem either stupid or green. He just wasn't listening very carefully. "Whether it's Navaja or some other leader, there's a gathering of Apaches out there," Blaine said curtly. "If you've been lookin' you've seen their smoke. They're probably watching us right now, they know who you are and how many and where you've come from. And they hadn't got around to bullets or arrows or knives with these pilgrims yet, but they would have. When they got tired of making sport of them."

Wilson's smile had vanished. "Just a minute, sir, you can't know—"

"I can. What you do with the information is your business."

"Where are you going?" Wilson said sharply as Blaine kneed his buckskin and swung away.

"That's my business," Blaine said.

"Hold it right there!" a harsh voice intruded. "You're not going anywhere."

Blaine felt sudden tension, memory noting the familiarity of that rasping voice before he placed it. Then a thin, wiry figure stepped out of the shadows of the veranda. He wore black gloves and carried a shotgun. It was aimed at Cullom Blaine's chest. He was dressed in black from boots to vest to expensive Stetson. His mouth was a tight, lipless line behind a drooping brown mustache, his eyes narrow slits of hatred.

"Who are you?" Lieutenant Wilson demanded.

"Marshal J. P. Holifield," the bristling little man snapped. "And that man is Cullom Blaine, wanted for murder and assaulting a peace officer!" He stepped from the veranda, the shotgun still trained carefully on Blaine. "Put your hands on the horn and climb down, Blaine, slow and easy. You're under arrest!"

The surprise he had felt when the marshal spoke lingered with Lieutenant Arnold Wilson as the small detachment of cavalry rode south. Theirs was a routine scouting mission, during which they had also provided escort for the widow of a late member of the 4th Cavalry, a young woman whom they had left behind at Cheever's Station to wait for the next stage. There had been no word of Apache uprisings in the territory. No wagon trains attacked, no isolated settlements burned out.

What bothered Arnold Wilson was that the man called Cullom Blaine had been so coolly certain. Nor was there anything excitable or alarmist about him. The opposite was true.

Wilson felt a trace of uneasiness. He was an ambitious young officer, eager to test himself and further his career here on the Western frontier. His personal experience of Indians was limited to last summer's skirmishes with Kiowa and Comanche renegades, as part of the campaign to make West Texas safe for settlers, and some fruitless chases after bands of raiders who had fled south of the border into Mexico. He was aware that Apache mavericks led by Navaja had also caused trouble the previous summer, striking in New Mexico and in West Texas before being chased northward into the Staked Plains. But that had ended when the young Apache slinked into the reservation with the coming of winter.

What Blaine had said about Navaja being on the loose

again seemed highly improbable. But if there were any possibility that Blaine was right, that the Apache outlaw was once again rounding up followers for a killing spree . . .

Wilson shook his head irritably. How could you give any credence to the word of a murderer? Wilson despised the rogues and outlaws who sometimes seemed to command unwarranted respect here in the West. But had he been too quick to lump Cullom Blaine among them? Blaine seemed a different type. Hard, yes, even hostile. But cool and steady, with a gaze that never wavered.

Reaching the spot he had taken note of that afternoon on the ride north, Lieutenant Wilson signaled for the patrol to stop and make camp. He was not really worried about the danger of Indian attack, but he had chosen a site that was on high ground with good cover, backed by impassable bluffs, and offering a commanding field of fire. There was also a trickle of water from an underground spring and a sheltered place with some grass near the foot of the bluffs to picket the horses. It was exactly what Wilson wanted for a campsite. He might have stayed at Cheever's Station for the night, but he preferred an open bivouac in the field, away from the station and its crowd of civilians. Besides, they had got in more than an hour's ride before light began to fail completely.

Beaver Sampson came up silently to Wilson's fire not long after the troopers had settled in. He squatted a little away from the fire and built a cigarette. When he had lit it with the glowing tip of a stick thrust into the fire, he said, "You doubled the watch."

"Yes," Wilson admitted.

"Good idea." Sampson was the civilian scout who had accompanied the detachment. He wasn't much to look at —bearded, a thin body that was all corded muscle, bright blue eyes that sometimes seemed a hundred years old, fringed leather pants and jacket blackened with age, an ancient smell about him of leather and tobacco and sweat (cavalry smells, Wilson thought)—but the young officer did not underestimate him. The scout was a seasoned veteran of the Indian wars. He had the reputation of knowing as much about Indians of the Southwest—Kiowas, Comanches and Apaches—as any man under Colonel Ranald Mackenzie's command.

"Why do you say that, Sampson?"

The tip of Sampson's cigarette glowed as he drew in smoke and filled his lungs before he spoke. "Blaine," he said.

"You know him?" Wilson said sharply.

The scout shook his head. "Heerd tell of him, though."

"You think there's something in what he said?" The lieutenant was very alert now. "About Navaja?"

Beaver Sampson shrugged. "What he said, Lieutenant . . . it's worth thinkin' about, anyways. Thing of it is, them pilgrims wasn't the only ones figgered the Apaches was out for blood. Blaine thought it too. And what I heerd about Blaine, he don't scare easy." The grizzled scout rose and turned away from the fire, his last words floating back out of darkness. "And he was right about that smoke."

For a long time Lieutenant Arnold Wilson stared into his small fire, thinking over Sampson's careful words, trying to recall exactly what it was about Cullom Blaine that seemed to give weight to his warning in spite of his dusty, nondescript appearance. Wilson was keenly aware that many a military career—or a life, for that matter—turned upon a small, seemingly insignificant decision or a careless misstep.

Might his ambition turn upon such an error? Could he have made a mistake about Cullom Blaine?

The officer stared out into the darkness of the broken plain.

5

Marshal J. P. Holifield had set a lantern on a stool at the far end of the stables near the big doorway. Through the open door of the cramped harness room in which he sat on the floor, awkwardly hunched against the wall, Blaine could see the glow cast by the lantern across the dirt floor, though not the lamp itself. Every once in a while Holifield moved across the path of light and a huge, grotesque shadow was thrown along the stables, spilling over the stalls and up the wall.

Blaine was tied hand and foot. "I'm taking no chances with you this time, Blaine," the marshal had said, grunting with the effort of tightening the rawhide strips he'd scrounged from Art Cheever's supplies. "This time you'll travel hog-tied."

"How will you explain it if I get shot on the way?"

Holifield slammed the back of his good hand across Blaine's face. "It'll come to me," he whispered hoarsely.

The bitterness and the long nursing of his hatred had eaten at Holifield, changing him. He wasn't as much the dandy as he had been when Blaine first cut his trail. The clothes were much the same, and he still favored black, but they weren't as clean and there were signs of wear along with old sweat stains. He had always been a bristling, feisty man, but there was something sour and mean about him that was more visible now, as if pain had scoured away any surface pleasantries.

"Yes, it hurts," Holifield said, as if reading Blaine's mind. He held up his right hand in its black leather glove. "Still hurts, especially when it's cold. Tells me when it's gonna rain, so I reckon you could say you did me a favor, Blaine."

Blaine was silent. No good reminding the marshal that he had forced the fight which resulted in bullets from Blaine's .44 Walker Colt smashing his gun hand and his right shoulder. Holifield hadn't wanted to listen to reason then and he wouldn't listen now.

Blaine shifted his weight, trying to ease some of the strain on his back. His hands were tied behind him, making it impossible to sit up straight or find any comfortable position. The leather strings dug into his wrists.

He heard a low voice and saw Holifield's shadow move quickly across the light. There was a murmured exchange, then a woman's voice rose, speaking more sharply. "He may be your prisoner, Marshal, but that's no reason to deny him food. From what I understand, he may have saved two lives today."

Blaine heard only the anger in Holifield's reply, not the words. But the woman was persistent, and a moment later Blaine heard footsteps moving toward him across the hard-packed floor. One of the half-dozen horses in the stables snuffled out of curiosity or restlessness, another stamped eagerly.

She stopped in the open doorway to the harness room, gazing down at Blaine with a frown. Blaine remembered seeing her on the veranda when he rode in that evening. He had thought her slender in that brief glance, but she didn't look as slight up close. There was, in fact, nothing fragile about her. Certainly not in the cool determination in her voice when she turned to the marshal and said, "I don't know how you expect a man to eat with his hands

tied behind him, Marshal. This is the same stew we all had.
It needs—"

"You can spoon it to him, Mrs. Allen," Holifield said
harshly. He stood close behind her with the lantern,
watching with wary suspicion. Maybe the marshal
thought she was going to cut him loose, Blaine thought.

The woman hesitated, looking from Blaine to the marshal and back again. "Very well," she said, "if that's the
way it has to be . . ." There was both disgust at the fool-
ishness of men and a quiet determination in her tone.

She took the cloth off the bowl she carried and a wave of
mingled smells made Blaine almost dizzy. He had eaten
nothing substantial in twenty-four hours, little enough
before that during several days' riding. When she knelt on
the floor beside him and began to spoon some of the
unidentified but savory mixture into his mouth, Blaine
wolfed it all down greedily. Only when she was scraping
the empty bowl with the spoon did he lean back with a
sigh and gaze directly into her eyes. "A tasty dish," he
said. "I won't ask what it was, if it was Cheever's woman
who made it. I'm obliged to you."

There was no amusement in the blue eyes or on her full-
lipped mouth. She regarded him with a quiet disdain.
"Don't misunderstand, Mr. Blaine. I hate everything you
stand for, the lawlessness you're so proud of out here in
the West, the violence and killing." She rose and stepped
back. "But I would not see anyone go hungry when there
is food to share."

He saw that she was a handsome woman, though not
quite as young as he had first thought, with a face not
cameo pretty but pleasant and alive, framed by a mass of
dusky blond hair, the color of sage honey, pinned into a
coil at the back of her neck. Close proximity made him
uncomfortably aware of the feminine swell of her hips

and bosom. A pleasant soapy scent lingered behind her in the close confines of the harness room. He returned her hostile gaze without expression, wondering what lay behind her outburst.

Holifield's rasping voice cut between them. "You've had your feed," he said to Blaine. "Be grateful for it. Now if you're finished, ma'am . . ."

There was a sudden commotion outside, along the wagon trail at the front of the station, a rumbling of iron-clad wheels, the rub and jingle of harness, and the slowing stamp of hoofs of many horses. Blaine heard a man call out, a quick exchange of voices, and then there was silence. The sounds told their own clear story of the arrival of the stage.

Holifield moved away to the front of the stables, leaving Blaine and the woman momentarily in darkness. He stirred and sensed her pulling back quickly. "Don't worry, Mrs. Allen," he said gently. "I don't bite, or do many of the other things I'm accused of."

She left without a word. Watching her move into the glow of the marshal's lantern until she was cut off from his view, Blaine found himself wondering what she was doing here at this remote outpost, alone, a woman with a wedding ring on her finger.

Walking across the yard toward the main station building, Jessica Allen was as puzzled by the man she had just left in the stables as he had been about her. She had sensed a deep anger in him, a coldness that was chilling, but there was also an unexpected calmness and dignity. In her mind, she realized, she had been quick to link him with the murderous scum who had killed Joseph Allen and left her a widow, an assessment based entirely on the marshal's harsh judgment. Alone in the stables with the

two men, Jessica had been startled to find that the evil she
had felt in that shadowy place was not in the man trussed
up in the small back room, but in the little lawman with
the lantern.

She shook off the impression. She knew nothing of the
man called Blaine, and a lawman in the West could not be
a gentle pacifist.

The reflection reminded her instantly of the Calders,
and when she stepped into the large main room of the
station house she immediately looked for Charity Calder.
There were a number of strangers in the station, apparently from the stage that had just pulled up, but Jessica
saw Charity watching her from a bench seat against the
far wall, her young husband beside her. With a smile Jessica crossed the room toward them.

"Your rescuer is fine," she said to the anxious young
woman. "Well enough to finish off a large bowl of stew." It
had, in fact, been Charity Calder's suggestion that the
prisoner in the stables should be given a meal.

"I still do not understand," Charity said. "I can't believe
what they say about him . . ."

"The marshal would not have arrested him without just
reason," Noah said soberly.

Charity Calder was not convinced. "I told thee how he
brought us here, Mrs. Allen, and how he could have shot
those Indians but did not, that he did no more than shoot
at the feet of their horses. Surely that tells something
about him. I cannot believe he is a bad man."

Jessica hesitated, then surprised herself by saying, "Life
is different in the West. Things aren't always what they
seem. Perhaps that is true of Mr. Blaine."

6

Cheever's Station was crowded that night. The stage had arrived late and would wait until first light before continuing west. Besides Clay Adams, the driver, and Ben Crisler, who rode shotgun for the stage, there were four passengers—an older couple, Fred and Mildred Sanderson, on their way to Santa Fe, whose dry climate was said to be beneficial to those with Fred's bronchial trouble; a drummer whose first interest was the bar Cheever had set up in one corner of the store side of the building; and a lean, sallow-faced man named Rimmer, who wore two six-guns in holsters tied to his legs. Rimmer said little to anyone but he seemed to take a particular interest in any talk about the marshal and his prisoner out in the stables.

One room, bare except for a number of cots, was set aside for travelers who wanted a bed for the night. The narrow beds rented for twenty-five cents a night including a blanket. Few women passed this way, and the room was usually able to accommodate as many men as were willing to pay to sleep under a roof. On this night, however, the room was set aside for the women only—Mildred Sanderson, Jessica Allen and Charity Calder. The men would have to fend for themselves, sleeping on the floor or one of the long benches in the main room. Art Cheever and his Kiowa wife, whom he called simply Woman, had their own small room at the back. Reno, Cheever's half-breed helper, who also had Kiowa blood, would rest on guard in the open by the corral, where the tired animals from the stage had been turned loose with most of the other horses, including the relief team that would pull the stage the next day. Marshal J. P. Holifield stayed close to his prisoner in the stables, hunched against a stall post, his baleful eyes on the dark doorway of the little room in which Blaine slept.

Noah Calder had been reluctant to be separated from his wife, but Charity had teased him with a gentle laugh. "It's just like it was in the village," she reminded him. "Would thee forget so soon? How at night we would take our separate stairways to bed, all the men and women apart, and thee were forbidden to take my hand or even to sit close to me?"

"Nay, I haven't forgotten. But it is different now."

"It is only for tonight, Noah."

Ben Crisler was a dour, taciturn man of forty with iron gray hair and beard, worn range clothes, and a battered hat in which the holes made in the crown by an Indian bullet entering and leaving were clearly visible. Crisler had a gimpy leg, another souvenir of a scrape with Comanches. An arrow had buried itself deep in the back of his leg just under the buttocks, chipping bone and tearing the big muscles of his thigh. It had left him crippled enough that the only job he had been able to hold since was riding shotgun on the stage, where he could sit favoring one side with a pillow under the other, and he didn't have to walk much or stay on his feet. Crisler hated Indians.

He had spent part of the evening killing half a bottle of raw whiskey with Clay Adams at Cheever's bar. Crisler liked Adams, an easygoing younger man who drove the stage, but he had got tired of listening to the talkative drummer who kept interrupting them, complaining about this godforsaken land where nobody would buy his cheap goods, everyone was thirsty, and there were too many ways to die. The drummer, whose name was Chandler, had the pink, clean-shaven face of a city man, and he smelled of scent. He also had long brown hair he was fond of combing carefully with his fingers. Crisler thought an Apache might drool over that hair.

Chandler started talking in a low voice about the young Shaker couple who had arrived at the station earlier that evening in their little wagon. "I heard about them back East," he confided. "They call 'em shaking Quakers back there, on account of the way they dance and shake themselves when they're having one of their meetings. Something peculiar about the way they carry on, what I heard."

"She's a pretty thing," Clay Adams murmured. A handsome man in a calico shirt, butternut trousers and half boots, Adams had an eye for the ladies, well aware that, when he walked across a room with his jaunty swagger, their eyes also followed him. "Shame she has to try to make herself as plain as a bedpost."

Chandler leaned toward him confidentially. "It's said they don't believe in a man and woman . . . uh . . . cohabiting," he said with a sly chuckle. "Even if they're man and wife."

Clay Adams pivoted halfway around to stare across the room at Noah Calder with an expression of incredulity. "You mean . . . he can't bed that pretty little girl? Now that's downright unnatural! A crying shame, that's what it is."

"I'm only saying what I heard."

"I've heard enough," Ben Crisler growled in disgust. He tossed down a last shot of whiskey and limped out of the station.

It was a dark night, clouds scudding swift and low over the flatlands and hunched over the shoulders of the bluffs to the north. A canyon that split those cliffs like the deep cut of an ax was as black as a mine shaft. Crisler stumbled in the dark as he made his way down to the pole corral behind the station buildings, just this side of the cottonwoods that marked the course of a shallow stream. Some crickets broke off their shrill singing, as if waiting for him to pass.

Crisler froze as he heard the sharp click of a rifle's hammer being thumbed to full cock. A shadow moved at the near corner of the corral. *"Quién es?"* a voice called softly.

"Take it easy," Crisler snapped back. "I'm with the stage, come to look after our horses." He felt a sting of anger in reaction to the quick jump of alarm. Reno, Cheever's stable hand, was part Indian, a wiry little man with dark brown skin, obsidian hair and eyes. The part that wasn't Indian, Crisler thought sourly, was Mexican.

"There is nothing to look after," Reno said with a soft laugh. "It is a quiet night."

Crisler grunted. "Maybe it won't stay that way. There's talk of Apaches on the loose." The Indian would know, he thought. They always did.

Crisler did not see the half-breed shrug. There was no purpose in worrying about what one could not change. "I do not think so," Reno said. "I have heard nothing, and the soldiers were here . . ." They would not have left so quickly, he seemed to imply, if there were any danger. It was the business of soldiers to kill Apaches, as it was the business of Apaches to kill soldiers.

"They're not here now," Crisler said darkly. "And if I

were you, I'd sleep with one eye open. Indians like to steal horses."

Reno chuckled. "But it is the way I always sleep."

Cullom Blaine slept fitfully, unable to find a comfortable position on the floor of the harness room, his mind busy examining and discarding a series of schemes and ruses that would somehow get him out of the predicament he was in. J. P. Holifield was not going to untie him, he had made that clear, and Blaine had about given up trying to twist his hands free of their rawhide bonds. All he had accomplished by his efforts was to wear off a layer of skin on his wrists.

He woke suddenly. It was the darkest hour before first light. The air was heavy, close, and he was sweating.

A man who rode the high line, and rode alone, learned to sleep lightly and awaken quickly. His senses were instantly alert; he didn't have to flog them into life.

The night was very still. Too quiet, Blaine thought. Even the crickets listened as he did, feeling danger in the air. It was the unnatural quiet that had pulled him abruptly out of sleep.

Blaine felt an uneasiness compounded by the fact that he was trussed up hand and foot, as helpless as a calf waiting for the branding iron. He was aware of the accepted wisdom that Apaches did not attack at night, fearing to wander lost in darkness if they should die in such a battle. It might be true as far as it went, but it left out the equally accepted wisdom that you could never be certain what an Apache might do. Especially one like Navaja, who flaunted any stereotypes.

Blaine hunched himself over to the open doorway and peered into the gloom of the stables. He hissed softly. "Marshal? You there, Holifield?"

There was no reply. After waiting a minute Blaine struggled to his feet, pressing his back against the wall and hitching upward a few inches at a time until he got his legs under him. There was just enough play in the leather around his ankles that he was able to shuffle awkwardly over to the narrow firing port. The opening was about a foot wide and four or five inches high.

At first there was only blackness. Then Blaine began to make out the shadowy depression where the stream ran, a few cottonwoods that clung to the bank, and the contours of the hills beyond them. He blinked and looked away, and when he looked back again he was able to see the frame of the corral and some dark shapes inside. A horse nickered nervously.

Blaine had been watching for about ten minutes when he heard the mournful hoot of an owl from the direction of the cottonwoods. It was the first natural sound to break the silence, and it came just when Blaine was about to admit that his imagination had been playing tricks with him. Peering into the dark until his eyes watered, he felt a fist of tension tighten its grip on his neck and shoulders.

Then a shadow melted and a dark figure rose straight up out of the ground near the corral and Blaine's heartbeat stumbled. "Holifield!" he yelled. "Goddam you, Marshal, wake up! They're after the horses!"

The warrior who was called The Knife had squirmed his way along a shallow wash from the banks of the stream toward the corral. The ditch was no more than six inches deep, it's sandy bottom pitted with gravel, but Navaja slithered along it like a brown snake, silent and invisible in the darkness of the overcast night.

At a corner of the corral he lay still. A man slept at the junction of poles directly ahead of him, about thirty feet away. He slept noisily with his mouth open, the Apache noted contemptuously. Navaja knew who he was, a man who was part Indian, of the Kiowa nation. The fact that they shared the color of their skin meant nothing to Navaja. A man who was not Apache was an enemy, one of many. In a few moments this one would sleep more quietly.

He also guarded the horses in the corral.

Navaja heard the low signal from the cottonwoods. Time to move quickly.

At the last moment Reno must have heard some small tick of sound through his cocoon of sleep. He jerked his head up and was alert enough to reach for the rifle at his side. But the sentry had slept too long and too carelessly. A band of iron clamped around his neck, dragging him down. Reno grabbed the muscular arm and tried to tear it free, at the same time kicking out frantically. The terrible pressure around his neck choked off any cry. He could smell the Apache—knew he should have smelled him sooner, that strong leathery odor of smoke and sweat and grime—and the smell more than anything else struck fear to the core of his brain.

The Apache's knife slid easily into the soft flesh of Reno's belly. Navaja drew it upward in a single swift stroke to a barrier of ribs, blood flowing warm on his hand. Reno's body bowed upward, bucking completely free of the ground. When he collapsed Navaja released his grip. The heavy blade flew in quick slashes around the enemy's skull as Navaja claimed his trophy. Then, bloody scalp in one hand, he was up and running swiftly toward the pole gate of the corral.

7

In the darkness and confusion Art Cheever blundered into someone and swore. A chair fell over with a clatter. From the sleeping room where the women were came a cry of alarm. A man struck a match and held it toward one of the coal-oil lamps and Cheever shouted, "Douse that light!"

At one of the firing ports just a few feet from Cheever a rifle crashed. Shrill yelps from outside punctuated a sudden rush of hoofs. By then Cheever had grabbed his rifle from behind the bar. He burst out onto the long veranda, levering a shell into the empty chamber as he moved. The rush of horses swept by on the east side of the station. Cheever knew there were Indians among them, had to be, but they were hanging so low over the horses they rode that he could not make them out in the whirl of running shapes. He held his fire, knowing it was useless.

Within seconds the Apaches and the bunch of stolen horses were gone, leaving behind only the drum of their hoofbeats fading off to the east. Art Cheever was aware of Ben Crisler beside him on the veranda, and of a chaos of cries and questions in the station behind them.

"I warned Reno," Crisler said sullenly.

Cheever felt a belated chill. *Where was Reno?*

The lawman who had been in the stables was at the corral ahead of them, kneeling beside the body on the ground. Cheever did not need to be told that Reno was dead. J. P. Holifield looked up at him, baring his teeth in a kind of snarl. "Took his scalp," he said.

Cheever waited for a stab of grief or loss. There was none. But there was something else: fear.

"Damn it all to hell!" Clay Adams swore. "They got every one of them horses!"

"There's a few safe in the stables," Ben Crisler said.

"One of 'em's mine," the marshal said curtly. "Another belongs to my prisoner."

Cheever did not answer, his mind already calculating his losses, a concern that momentarily overrode his fear. The other horses under roof were his own. Most of those taken—fifteen, according to his close reckoning—belonged to the stage line. Only one of his horses had been stolen, along with two lame mounts left behind to rest by the cavalry. The Apaches, finding them lame, would almost certainly eat them. Cheever scowled. The army might try to hold him accountable. Any time you dealt with the government you came up on the short end.

"At least they're gone," Clay Adams said. It required a young man's optimism to surface so quickly after another's death. "It could have been worse."

"Don't bet on it," Cheever said gloomily, staring off to the east where the Apaches had disappeared with their prizes of war. The first pale rim of light defined the black edge of the plain.

"It was only the horses they were after," Adams protested.

"Maybe," Cheever said. He stared down at Reno's body with its crimson cap where the hair had been. Where the hell was he going to find another good stable hand? Especially one who would work for next to nothing. "If it was Navaja, he might not be satisfied." He wouldn't be, Cheever knew, the fear nibbling at him again.

They all assembled in the main room of the station, Marshal Holifield having brought his prisoner up from the stables as a precaution. One man was posted at the back with a view of the stables, but even Cheever admitted to himself that if the Apaches wanted to attack the station and steal the remaining horses under cover of that attack, it might prove hard to stop them. The group of defenders was too small to be split between the station and the stables.

With the dawn the sky remained a leaden gray; a heaviness in the air promised more rain. The gloom seeped into the station where there was a prevailing mood of apprehension.

Several running arguments added to the uneasy atmosphere. Ray Chandler, the drummer, demanded that the stage leave at once before there was more trouble. The belligerent marshal having testily refused to give up his and his prisoner's horses, Clay Adams argued that Cheever should lend his four remaining horses to the stage line. Although the stage had arrived with a team of six, four could do the pulling. But Cheever resisted the idea of being left without a horse of his own as long as maverick Apaches were on the prowl.

"The eastbound stage should be through here tomorrow," Adams insisted. "You can send word on with the driver, and I'll carry the same message. You'll get your horses back."

"If you get through," Cheever said darkly. "And the eastbound stage gets here."

"Why wouldn't they? Them Apaches wanted horses, that's all."

"No," the man in the corner said quietly. "They'll be back."

Everyone stared at Cullom Blaine. The marshal had released the rawhide strips around Blaine's ankles when he led his prisoner from the stables, but Blaine's wrists remained bound. He was sitting on the end of a long bench in the back corner near the bar, placed where Holifield could watch him and he was a long way from a door or window.

"You can't know that," Clay Adams said uncertainly.

Blaine shrugged. "You didn't listen to me yesterday, and it's up to you what you do today. But if you try to take that stage through, with just you and a man ridin' shotgun, you'll lose more than horses."

"Shut your mouth, Blaine," the marshal said.

"Why should he?" Art Cheever said. "He's right."

"You jest don't want us to pull out and leave you here alone," Adams said.

They were interrupted by Woman, bringing a steaming pot of coffee from the kitchen. After helping himself to a mug of the hot, welcome brew Clay Adams took up his argument. "What makes you so certain they'll be comin' back?"

"They want something else," Blaine said.

"What?" young Adams demanded. "Do you know somethin' you're not telling?"

Blaine shrugged. "Maybe they need guns."

Cheever's quick glare was oddly hostile. "What makes you say that?"

"Indians always need guns and ammunition. Coming off the reservation, Navaja would be no exception."

But Cheever, who had a surly temper at the best of times, angrily brushed aside the suggestion. "If it's Navaja out there, he don't need a reason to come back. Nothin' more than us bein' here . . . and women amongst us."

The thin, sallow-faced Rimmer surprised everyone

when he spoke. "You should listen to him." He nodded toward Blaine. "And maybe the marshal should think about cuttin' him loose and givin' him a gun before the Apaches get here, because there won't be time to think about it then. And we'll need every man who can shoot."

This quiet pronouncement brought a long silence to the room. "I'll take my chances with Navaja," Holifield said flatly, "before I'll put a gun in Blaine's hand."

"Maybe *you* would," Rimmer answered. "You ain't alone. If the Apaches come, we'll need him."

The attack came without warning. Apaches frequently struck at first light, hoping to catch their enemies asleep. Navaja had waited three hours into the day, long enough for those inside the station to be lulled into a false sense of security, to become careless and lazy-eyed.

One minute the terrain surrounding the station was empty of life. The next moment muscular brown bodies erupted from the ground as if emerging from holes like prairie dogs. The people in the station had become so relaxed that two men were caught outside. One was Fred Sanderson, trapped in the narrow box of the outhouse in back of the main building. The door was closed and he stood inside shaking with fright, waiting for the door to burst open. Apparently the Apaches had failed to see him take the short walk from the station to the outhouse. Through the fury of the first attack and the long hour of sporadic shooting that followed, Sanderson remained where he was, cowering in terror. The door never opened.

Ben Crisler was caught at the stage, and he had been seen. Adams had pulled up along the west side of the station building the evening before. Crisler was no more than fifteen feet from the corner of the veranda when he saw an Apache running low toward the stagecoach. Two other braves veered toward him. Crisler was carrying his Winchester and he snapped off a quick shot that missed. Then he ran for the veranda.

He didn't make it.

There was a crackle of rifle fire like corn popping from both inside and outside the station. Ben Crisler never heard the shot that brought him down. A bullet caught him in the leg and dropped him as if he'd been roped. His head and shoulder slammed into the edge of the veranda, stunning him. Rough hands grabbed him and dragged him over behind the coach. As he came to and began to struggle, mind dark with rage, something clubbed him over the head and the dark turned crimson.

Most of the men within Cheever's Station had lived a long time in the West. They were handy with rifle and six-shooter, they had shot buffalo and deer and other game, and they had fought Indians before. Chandler and Sanderson had been Union soldiers. Only Noah Calder was a stranger to gunfire. Consequently the response to the attack was quick and cool. The shutters at the few windows had earlier been closed and barred. There were narrow loopholes on all sides and in the kitchen at the back. The small room in which Cheever and Woman slept had no window or port—nor, Cheever said, did a small padlocked storage room. The communal sleeping room had only one window facing the stables. Rimmer took that stand, a choice that proved fortunate. Early in the fighting an Apache tried to reach the stable doors. Rimmer's rifle shot cut him down. He lay there through most of the fighting. Toward the end another brave made it to the doors and dragged them open while Rimmer was returning fire from another quarter. Rimmer snapped a shot without aiming and saw the Indian stumble before he vanished inside the stables.

The attack came so suddenly that there was no time to pursue the quarrel over cutting Cullom Blaine loose. He remained where he was in the corner, hands tied behind him, fingers numb from the long hours during which the narrow strips of leather had bitten into his flesh.

Early on, in the first scramble to cover every side of the station with adequate fire, Cheever had thrust a rifle toward Noah Calder. "Cover that side window!" he barked.

Noah shook his head helplessly. "Nay, friend . . . uh . . . I'm sorry, but I can't."

"What do you mean you can't?" Cheever roared.

"I don't believe in killing."

"What's that got to do with anythin'? Godalmighty, man, do you believe in gettin' killed? Get out of the way then—over with the women!"

Noah huddled in the corner with Charity, feeling a confusion that was new to him. Everyone in the station was clearly threatened—one, at least, the man who rode with the stage, already taken by the Indians. Noah was accustomed to a communal life in which everyone took part, sharing every burden. No one shirked. Now his refusal to fight alongside the others added to their danger.

"It doesn't seem right," he said to Charity. "They try to protect us, and I can do nothing."

"It is what thee believes, Noah."

"Yes, I know . . ."

He saw the stagecoach driver, Clay Adams, at the front window, firing his rifle until it was empty, then setting it aside and taking up a six-gun to continue his fire, all the while grinning with a kind of savage joy. He was a young man filled with life, he did not seem a bad man. How was it that he could feel such joy in battle while Noah, who refused to fight, felt only misgivings?

Even the widow, Jessica Allen, took part, at first going from one stand to another to reload weapons for the men, and then, when the Apaches made a rush at the front of the station, leaping to one of the front firing ports with one of Cheever's loaded rifles.

It ended as suddenly as it had begun. Driven back from the veranda, the Apaches simply melted away. There was a long period of stunned silence, while the people inside Cheever's Station turned to stare at each other. In the silence Mildred Sanderson was heard sobbing, and it was only then that most of them realized Sanderson was nowhere to be seen. "He was outside," the woman sobbed. "He's dead, I know he's dead!"

And at that moment there was a long-drawn-out, inhuman scream from outside. Mildred Sanderson came to her feet with a cry.

"That ain't him," Art Cheever said grimly. "That was Ben."

No one said anything. They would find Ben Crisler later, tied spread-eagled to one of the wheels of the stagecoach on the side away from the station where the Apaches had been able to work on him in safety. He had taken a long time to die.

During that moment of silence while the echo of Crisler's dying scream seemed to shiver in the air, Fred Sanderson burst through the door and collapsed on the floor.

This time no one believed the Apaches had gone for good. They had lost three, perhaps four men, though only the one Rimmer had dropped in the open by the stable doors, and another Cheever had shot just steps from the veranda, were known to be dead. Both bodies had disappeared when the Apaches withdrew. Two or three others may have been wounded, one of them the brave Rimmer had shot as he entered the stables. A careful search of the stables proved fruitless, however, only a few spots of blood on the floor showing that the Apache had been there and that he was hurt.

Except for Ben Crisler the defenders had escaped serious injury. Clay Adams, his left shoulder burned by a bullet, and Cheever, who had had a splinter of wood driven into his cheek, were still fit to fight.

"Next time they'll be more careful," Cheever said. The younger and more reckless ones, willing to take chances, were already dead or wounded. The seasoned warriors would be more careful. "They'll be out there but you won't see 'em."

"Next time we need every hand we've got," Rimmer said. His cold glance found Noah Calder. "I don't know what your excuse is, but it don't hold. You'll use a gun or I'll break one around your neck."

"Nay, friend, I cannot."

"You can't order anyone what to do," Jessica Allen said, not flinching when Rimmer wheeled on her. "Not to go against what they believe."

Rimmer held her eyes for a long moment with an icy stare that caused her to repress a shiver. Then he gave an elaborate shrug and turned slowly toward J. P. Holifield. "Marshal, your prisoner don't have no excuse. If he's the catamount you seem to think he is, he can fight Apaches. He won't be runnin' anywheres."

"That's for me to say."

"You don't cut him loose," Rimmer said easily, "I will."

Watching and listening, Cullom Blaine wondered who Rimmer was. The twin six-shooters tied low against his thighs told plainly enough *what* he was. But why was he here? What had a gunfighter been doing on the stage? And why was he so interested in Blaine?

The taut confrontation ended unexpectedly. "I'll turn him loose," the marshal said grudgingly. "I don't want to end up like Ben Crisler any more than the rest of you. But he stays close to me where I can watch him. And if he makes a wrong move, I'll shoot him, Apaches or no Apaches!"

8

Nothing happened through the middle of the day. Shortly after noon the rain came, hard enough to make the dust bounce in small, silent explosions on the wagon road that ran in front of Cheever's Station. The canyon to the north was filled with gray mist, and the ridgetops were lost in the heavy rain clouds. The dry washes that ran away from the hills quickly filled with rushing water.

Cullom Blaine was stationed at one of the loopholes on the west side of the main room of the station, where Marshal Holifield could man another opening and still keep an eye on him. At noon Charity Calder brought him some stringy, unidentifiable meat and warm bread. She kept her eyes averted and would not have spoken had not Cheever and Clay Adams tramped into the station after rescuing Ben Crisler's dead body from the wheel of the stagecoach. The two men were grimly silent. The young woman watched them with horror in her eyes. "How could they . . . those savages . . . do such a thing?" she whispered.

Though she had not meant her words for Blaine, he answered them. "They don't see things the same as you or I do. What to you seems cruel and barbaric, to the Apache is an accepted part of his life."

"Torturing a man? And taking his scalp? No wonder they are called savages!"

"An Apache would expect the same from his enemy. He

would be surprised if it didn't come. Torture gives an enemy the chance to show his courage, even in death. Fighting, and dying in battle if it comes to that, gives the Apache the same chance. Not that he's any more eager to die than anyone else. He's a warrior, a fighting man, and a proud one."

"I don't understand such a man."

"He wouldn't understand if you tried to explain to him what the Bible says about turning the other cheek."

Charity Calder turned away abruptly. "I don't wonder that thee defends him," she said, "if it is true what they say about thee."

Blaine could not blame her. She had certainly heard the whispered questions and conversations about him among the others at the station. He was a hunted man, an outlaw, and a murderer. The young woman—hardly more than a child—had come from a place where she had been taught that all violence was wrong. What would she make of a murderer except that he had to be the devil's companion? And how could she be expected to grasp the Apache's view of life, even more alien to her experience?

The heavy rain lasted less than an hour. It diminished to scattered showers, the clouds broke up, and a rainbow arced through the mist as the sun peered through. Everything had a startling clarity and vividness, the air washed clean by the rain. Inside the station it was quiet after the noisy downpour, and it soon began to turn hot and muggy.

As the afternoon wore on Blaine sensed an easing of the tension in the station. He did not relax his own alert watch. He was a patient man, like most who had long lived close to nature and to danger, and he had learned not to spend too much time anticipating what could not be predicted. All he knew for certain was that the danger was not over.

Something about the Apache attack was bothering him, but he could not exactly put his finger on it. Thinking back on the morning's attack, it seemed to him there had been surprisingly little gunfire from the Indians after the first savage fighting. A war of attrition was not unknown to the Indians, a slow wearing down of the enemy—the Apache too was infinitely patient—but such a tactic did not seem a particularly effective one against Cheever's Station, where the defenders had good cover, food and water, and apparently plenty of weapons and ammunition. What was Navaja after? Was he trying to lure the soldiers from Fort Tracy into a trap? Was his own force strong enough for that? Or was there something else behind the assault on Cheever's Station?

Cullom Blaine had a hunch Art Cheever might be able to give an answer.

"It isn't right," Noah Calder argued to Charity. "It's not right that I should do nothing while others defend us."

"We do not believe in killing, Noah. Thee cannot doubt that."

"I am not so certain anymore . . ."

"Mother Ann taught against violence, or any deed that would harm another."

"There is no dust in heaven," Noah murmured.

"What did thee say?"

"Mother Ann thought all the world must be clean," Noah said. "We know that it is not always so, and not always bad on that account. She also forbade man and woman being together . . ."

Charity was silent for a moment, her face coloring visibly. "One transgression does not condone another."

"Does thee really believe we transgressed?" Noah pressed her. "Nay, I do not believe it is so. I cannot believe thee would have come with me knowing it to be against God."

"What does thee say, Noah?"

"Only that we must think on these things ourselves. If it's right for us to be together as man and woman, and I do not doubt it, may not other teachings be questioned, too?"

"It cannot be right to kill another."

"But it is right then to be killed? That is what yon friend asked of me. Would it be right for me to let those savages capture thee? I cannot believe that."

Charity studied him anxiously, perplexed and worried by his arguments, for she could not find certain answers to them. She glanced across the room at the man called Blaine, who had rescued them from the Apaches not twenty-four hours ago. She remembered again the strength and assurance she had felt in him, and the intuitive perception that he had led them to the safety of Cheever's Station even though—contrary to what he said —he had not been coming this way. Led them to safety and himself into danger, she thought. For if he had not brought them here he would not have been made prisoner by the marshal.

Yet she had judged him as harshly as she did the Apaches.

In that moment Charity felt the slipperiness of moral judgments. "I don't know," she said. "I don't know . . ."

Art Cheever unlocked the storeroom behind the bar, carefully closing the door behind him. He emerged moments later with three Sharps carbines, single-shot breechloaders, and several boxes of ammunition. He padlocked the heavy wooden door once more.

Cullom Blaine watched thoughtfully as Cheever passed out ammunition. He received one of the Sharps carbines and set it on the floor alongside his own Winchester, beside the loophole where he watched and waited. An extra rifle, even a scarred old single-shot, was welcome, and the Sharps was both durable and reliable.

He wondered how many others like it Cheever had in his locked storeroom.

Cheever . . . Rimmer . . . Holifield . . . Sanderson . . . Calder . . . each seemed to have his personal agenda. The drummer had fought surprisingly well, as had Clay Adams. But the group was not one Cullom Blaine would have chosen to have at his side when making a stand against renegade Apaches. Still, no man always got to choose when or where he would come up against danger or death, or who would be beside him.

He thought of the soldier's widow from Fort Tracy. She had done well, too. Looking up, he found Jessica Allen watching him.

They struck again at dusk, when the light for shooting was poorer and the men inside the station were just about played out from the long afternoon of waiting. This time there was no all-out assault. Instead there was accurate, deliberate fire from points scattered all around Cheever's Station—from the corral and the banks of the stream to the south, from the cover of rocks on all sides, from the canyon across the way, and even from points high up on the steep bluffs to the north. It was not safe to stand in front of a shuttered window or too near one of the narrow slits that served as firing ports for those in the station. Bullets whined and thudded and bit off splinters of wood, and occasionally found a gap.

One bullet found an opening in the front, sang across the room unimpeded, and smashed one of the bottles behind Cheever's bar, spraying whiskey and glass.

Another hit Fred Sanderson, nervously stationed at one of the loopholes on the east side of the building. He saw no one, heard nothing, before the bullet struck his collarbone, smashing it, and, its course diverted, tore out a chunk from the side of his neck, which bled profusely. The bloody wounds, which looked more deadly than they proved to be, brought instant hysteria to his wife, a plump and pleasant woman who was suddenly out of her element.

Blaine helped carry Sanderson away from his post and found Jessica Allen immediately beside him, using a strip torn from her dress to staunch the bleeding. He watched her for a moment, silent. Then he returned to his own post and picked up his rifle.

Holifield glared at him from his spot next to the nearest window. "This don't change a thing, Blaine," he said. "When this is over you'll still go back with me, and you'll hang."

"For what, Marshal?" Blaine answered him harshly. "For killing the snakes who set fire to my house and my wife inside it? For going after the men who watched her burn? Where are you gonna find the jury in Texas that will hang me for that, Holifield?"

Holifield flushed with anger. "You don't make your own law, Blaine. Don't set yourself up as no righteous man what done no wrong!"

A flicker of movement in the brush caught Blaine's full attention. He fired into the brush but sensed even as he squeezed the trigger that he was too late. He said no more to Holifield, even regretting his brief outburst. The marshal was not a man to reason with.

No shot had answered Blaine's. The Apaches were not wasting ammunition, he thought, and the usual assumption would have been that they could keep this up for a long time, pinning the defenders down inside the station, wearing them down, picking them off one by one. But even before dark came the shooting had fallen off, only an occasional random bullet smacking into wall or shutter.

Then it was dark and the firing ceased.

Clay Adams voiced the questions that were in everyone's mind. "Why didn't they rush us? What are they up to? D'you think maybe they're pullin' out?"

For a while no one spoke. There was the flare of a match and Art Cheever lit one of the coal-oil lamps in the main room. His gaunt face brooded in the shadows as he turned away from the light. "They don't have ammunition, is my guess."

"What makes you say that?" Marshal Holifield demanded suspiciously. He too had been entertaining questions about Cheever's storeroom and what it might hold.

"They didn't do much shootin', did they?"

"Is that all you know?"

Cheever lifted his stooped shoulders in a shrug. "What else would there be?"

"Maybe you should tell us," Cullom Blaine drawled. "Maybe we ought to know why, first thing out of the box, Navaja had his bunch head straight for Cheever's Station."

9

"You'll open up that storeroom of yours," the man called Rimmer said quietly to Cheever, "or I'll put a hole in you first and the door second."

"Hold on!" Cheever blustered. "You got no call—"

"I'd do it," Cullom Blaine suggested quietly. "He means what he says."

Rimmer gave Blaine a wolfish grin. He held out his left hand toward Cheever while his right hand hovered over the butt of the six-shooter strapped to his leg. "Man makes sense, you oughta listen to him. I'll take them keys."

"No need for that," Cheever said truculently. "I'll open up."

There was a general movement closer to the bar and the door behind it that led into the dark, narrow storeroom. Rimmer shouldered past Cheever after he unlocked the door. He peered inside, then gestured impatiently. "Gimme that lamp." Several of the onlookers craned their necks to see into the storeroom as Rimmer held up the coal-oil lamp.

He turned back into the main room with a tight grin, holding up what looked like a new Colt revolving-cylinder carbine, a sheen of oil visible on the barrel and cylinder. "There's half a box of these in there, spankin' new." There was a dangerous glitter in his eyes as he glared at Cheever. "Reckon maybe you figured on startin' your own war."

"I bought them guns from the gov'ment," Cheever said quickly. "I got the bill of sale to prove it."

"I don't give a holler in hell how you got 'em!" Rimmer snarled. "You been sellin' guns to the Indians—guns they're usin' to kill white folks!"

Cheever's face had paled under the leathery folds, but he stood his ground. "You think the gov'ment would've sold 'em to me if I was sellin' to the Indians?"

"Maybe they didn't know."

"They'd know soon enough." Cheever looked around for support, his gaze fastening on Marshal Holifield. "Those guns are for sale to white men," he said. "Settlers and drifters, prospectors, cowhands, whatever, they stop here for flour and food, and for guns and ammunition and other supplies. Even the peaceable Indians do some tradin'. But I'm a law-abidin' man, Marshal. You can ask the army. They'll tell you."

Holifield regarded him suspiciously for a moment before he spoke. Then he said, "Would Navaja know you have guns? Even if you don't sell to Indians? If you been dealing in rifles, I reckon any Apache who wanted to know could find it out."

Cheever checked a quick reply. Holifield's question had given him a reprieve. "I wouldn't know about that. I suppose . . . it's possible, sure."

"You suppose!" Rimmer said scornfully. "I oughta put a bullet in you right now."

"There'll be no shooting in here," Marshal Holifield bristled.

Rimmer regarded him with his tight, nasty smile.

"There's no proof Cheever has been sellin' guns to the Apaches," Holifield said coldly. "I wouldn't put it past him, but there's no provin' it. And unless you got somethin' to offer besides wild talk, that's the end of it."

There was a long moment of silence before Rimmer's smile widened, though it did not extend as far as his eyes. "You're the lawman here, Marshal. If that's the way you call it . . ." He shrugged. "I'm not one to buck the law."

Listening to the exchange, Cullom Blaine wondered if he was the only one to catch the hint of mockery behind Rimmer's words.

Only a few minutes later Rimmer approached Holifield again. "I been thinkin', Marshal. One of them Apaches might have got into the stables."

Holifield's gaze was sharp. "Why didn't you say somethin' before?"

"I wasn't sure—still don't know for certain. But we know they's after our horses. During the first fracas I cut a couple of 'em down tryin' to get into the stables. I been thinkin' Navaja would want one of his braves in there. Might've done it during this last attack."

"If one of 'em's in there," Clay Adams burst out, "we got to smoke him out!"

"No need to send our whole army outside," Rimmer said easily, still addressing his thoughts to Holifield. "You and me could handle it, with your prisoner. The rest could cover us, make sure the Apaches don't make another run at us."

"I told you before," the marshal said suspiciously. "I don't send Blaine outside with a gun."

Rimmer smiled. "He don't have to carry iron, Marshal. We just put him on point, send him through them doors first. If there's an Apache in there, we'll know it soon enough."

Slowly J. P. Holifield's suspicion faded from his eyes. His gaze flicked toward Blaine with a glint of amusement. "You got any objections, Blaine?"

"Would it make any difference?"

"I reckon not."

"Then why are you asking?"

The marshal bit down, his face pinching with hostility. "No reason—no reason at all. You'll go out there, Blaine, you'll go through those doors and I'll be right behind you. Make one wrong move and even the Apaches won't want you. You'll be buzzard bait!"

When they had gone out, moving single file through the darkness toward the stables, Clay Adams watched from just inside the kitchen door, wishing that he had been chosen to go with them. The exhilaration of the fighting lingered in his mind. It wasn't that he liked killing, he thought. It was just that there was no other feeling like that high excitement of the battle, the jolt of panic as death charged right at you on a pony, the shock of pleasure as the rifle butt kicked against your shoulder and the dark face of terror disappeared from your sights.

Not even a woman could give you that, he thought. Not even a woman like that young ripe widow, or the little Shaker girl with the pretty face . . .

Cullom Blaine knew something was wrong, and he wondered that J. P. Holifield did not sense it. His hatred blinded him, Blaine thought. It twisted his thinking and left him blind to things he would otherwise have questioned.

Rimmer had cut them both out of the herd. He had done it cleverly, playing on the marshal's hostility toward his prisoner. But it was obvious to Blaine what he was doing, and it should have been obvious to the suspicious Holifield. If only he weren't so full of hate . . .

The passionate bonds that tied Blaine and Holifield to-

gether stretched back over the months and years, all the
way back to the brutal slaying of Blaine's wife, Samantha,
by a gang of robbers. Consumed with grief and rage, Cullom Blaine had vowed to hunt down each of her killers. It
was his pursuit of one of them, Lem Seevers, that had
brought Blaine up against J. P. Holifield.

Seevers had taken refuge at a notorious robbers' roost
called Price's Landing, so named after the most dangerous curly wolf of the bunch, Sam Price. Holifield had been
giving the badmen of Price's Landing a hard time, lying in
wait for some of them coming and going. And it was said
that, once in Holifield's custody, an outlaw had about as
much chance of surviving to stand trial as a biscuit in
gravy.

J. P. Holifield was a stubborn, mean-spirited man, and
when Blaine went into the hideout after Seevers, the marshal lumped him in with the outlaws and thieves he despised. He would never see it another way. Convinced
that Blaine was on the dodge, he jumped him when he left
the Landing. Before the confrontation ended, the
lawman's deputy—what was his name? Armstrong?
Blaine was startled at how completely he had forgotten
the young deputy—was wounded, and Holifield himself
put out of commission by two lucky shots that smashed his
shoulder and right hand, permanently crippling him.

By engineering that shootout, Holifield had pushed
Cullom Blaine over the narrow line that divided a hunter
from an outlaw. From that time on Blaine's long quest had
taken a different turn. He rode outside the law, a man
who had locked away his past and cared nothing for the
future, a hunter who lived only to find and face down the
killers who had destroyed everything he had—the gunman, Abe Stillwell, who was still laughing at the grim-
faced rancher who had challenged him when Blaine's

bullet cut him down; Lem Seevers, shot as he tried to escape from Price's Landing; Ned Keatch, who had tried unsuccessfully to hide from Blaine in the confusion of a range war.

Others still survived. The skull-faced Wes Hannifan and his wily sidekick, Tinker Wright. And the Clancy brothers, Tom and Art, who had ended up in Huntsville Penitentiary for stealing Blaine's horses, though they were never convicted of their greater crime of murder.

Which of them had hired Rimmer?

"Hold it, Blaine!" Rimmer hissed softly. Blaine stopped in front of the stable doors, one of which hung open about a foot. Inside it was dark as a root cellar. "Have him go in first, Marshal."

Holifield, carrying a sawed-off shotgun, was close behind Blaine and to his left. Rimmer was off to the right, armed with the Colt carbine he had taken from Cheever's storeroom as well as the twin six-guns he wore. He moved in closer as Blaine reached for the half-open door.

There was a faint creak as the door swung toward him. Instinctively Cullom Blaine braced against the impact of a bullet or an arrow. He stood in the doorway, unarmed, knowing that he would be clearly visible against the night sky to anyone hiding in the darkness of the stables.

Nothing happened. From inside the building came a rustling sound. One of the horses shifting weight, turning toward the open door. Blaine saw the white gleam of an eye.

"Inside, Blaine," Holifield ordered quietly.

He was close, and Blaine wondered if this was the time for him to make his play, if there would ever be a better time. But out of the corner of his eye he saw Rimmer edging nearer. Blaine might get the jump on one man, not on two.

Blaine stepped inside the stables.

He knew right away that there was no Apache warrior lurking in the shadows. If there had been one, he would have had ample warning. There was no back door, but there were shutters opening out off the loft at the back of the building. Chances were the Indian had not even waited long enough to be forced to escape that way.

It occurred to him that Rimmer had been the last one watching the stables as darkness came and the fighting ceased. Rimmer knew—

Blaine whirled. J. P. Holifield had followed him into the stables, sticking close, and Rimmer had entered behind them. As Blaine turned, an alarm bell ringing in his brain, Rimmer stepped away from the open doorway into blackness. The marshal grunted in edgy surprise but it was Blaine's movements that held his attention. "What the hell—"

Flame spurted out of the blackness behind him, and the stables were filled with the roar of a six-shooter and the bite of gunpowder. The feisty little lawman grunted again, an explosion of breath as if he had been kicked. Blaine heard him floundering like a man whose boot skates on ice. He was trying to lift the shotgun he carried with his good left hand, but it was as if the weapon were too heavy for him. The barrel tilted down toward the floor, and the marshal followed it, tumbling onto his face.

All this happened while Blaine was heeling around. He dropped into a crouch near the fallen marshal but Rimmer bit off a savage command. "Back off, Blaine! Do it quick or you take a lead pill in the belly!"

For a moment the two men confronted each other in the dimness, Blaine's hand only a foot from the shotgun Holifield had dropped. He knew he would never be able to reach it in time, not with Rimmer's six-shooter aimed at his middle.

Slowly Cullom Blaine stood erect. Rimmer dropped his revolver into its holster and smoothly brought the carbine's muzzle to bear, the weapon cocked and ready. "Turn around!" he barked.

"Why'd you gun him down?" said Blaine over his shoulder as he obeyed. "Who are you?"

"Does it matter? One way or another, you're a dead man, Blaine. If it wasn't me it would've been the marshal there. Or somebody else." He gave a soft, humorless chuckle. "You'd be dead now, Blaine, partners with the marshal, if it wasn't that the price goes higher if I turn you over alive."

"You're a bounty hunter."

"Some old friends of yours'll be joinin' us soon. They want you bad enough old Navaja and his braves won't scare 'em off. And they got the gold to pay for you. If they'd got to you first, I'd be a poorer man."

"The Clancy boys," Blaine said softly.

There were voices outside the stables. Someone called out worriedly, "What's goin' on in there? Marshal Holifield?"

Blaine heard the slide of Rimmer's boots on the dirt floor and he tried to duck away as Rimmer flipped the carbine over in his hands and chopped down with the wooden stock. The blow grazed Blaine's head and slammed into his shoulder, momentarily paralyzing him. He kicked out but his leg moved as if it were in water. Then Rimmer struck again, and this time he laid the stock hard across Cullom Blaine's skull and Blaine plummeted into a deeper blackness.

He swam out of it briefly, hearing the excited questions muffled, as if they came to him filtered through the dark blanket covering him. He felt the hard dirt of the stable floor, the grit of straw against his face, the pain racketing through his skull. He tried to move, clawing for the surface of consciousness, and Rimmer said clearly, "He snakebit the marshal. Jumped him and grabbed his six-gun. Holifield never got to use that sawed-off gun of his, Blaine was too quick, I reckon."

"Is the marshal . . . ?"

"Shot him dead 'fore I could stop him. Good thing I was able to get to him quick as I did, or he'd be loose."

Groggily Blaine understood why Rimmer had used his six-gun instead of the carbine to drop Holifield. It was the only way he could shift the blame. Blaine wanted to shout, "He's lying! Listen to him—can't you hear the lie?" But the blanket seemed to be stuffed into his mouth and no sound came out.

"Shot him in the back, that's what he done!" Rimmer snarled.

The hard toe of his boot slammed into the side of Cullom Blaine's head, and the blackness buried him.

10

Mildred Sanderson was a plump, agreeable, graying woman in her forties. In her own element she was a friendly, even kindly sort, but now there was a hurt, bewildered look in her eyes, as if life had struck her too many blows. Fred's illness was one of them. A life that had seemed settled, orderly, predictable, had been turned upside down. They had had to leave Pittsburgh, where both had lived all their lives, where they had worked and played, made friends, raised two children—both grown now. Mildred had expected to stay there for the rest of her life, bouncing grandchildren on her knee, gossiping with old friends, watching the leaves change color on trees she had known since she was a child. Now she would have none of that. Fred needed a warm, dry climate. If they stayed, the doctor had said, Fred would not live long.

No one had told her that where they were going Fred might be struck down by an Indian's bullet. That life here in the West would never be as safe and predictable as the life she and Fred had known. Mildred felt terribly isolated and vulnerable. Nothing was familiar, not the people, the dangers, the food, even the land, which was raw and pitiless. Its immensity terrified her. That bloodthirsty savages could erupt out of that wilderness was even more terrifying.

And what if Fred's wound—he had bled so much—what if he . . .

"He's going to be fine," Jessica Allen said, as if reading the older woman's mind. She spoke in a soothing, reassuring tone which Mildred recognized as one she might have used with one of the children who'd scraped a knee or cut a hand. Mildred suddenly felt ashamed of her earlier outbursts. The sight of all that blood pouring from Fred's neck had unraveled her. "Mr. Sanderson is resting. Why don't you get some sleep?"

"I couldn't," Mildred said. "Indians . . . murderers . . . I couldn't close my eyes."

Jessica smiled. She was a friendly, comforting woman, Mildred thought. And she had known grief enough of her own, for someone so young. "Why don't you try? Nothing's going to happen now. The men think the Apaches have gone. There's a good chance the eastbound stage will get through in the morning, and there'll be more people on it. There might even be a troop escorting the stage. They do that if they believe there's any danger."

Mildred Sanderson, protesting mildly, allowed herself to be led to one of the narrow beds in the sleeping room, though she knew she wouldn't dare close her eyes. She lay back, thinking suddenly and with a searing intensity of longing of her old room with the flowered wallpaper and the cannonball four-poster bed, the marble-topped dresser against the wall to the left of the window, and the way the sun would slant through the curtains in the morning . . .

"To come all this way," she whispered, so low that Jessica had to lean forward to hear her. "Fred could die before we get out of here." Her voice rose. "We came all this way so he could live a better life, and now this! It's not right!"

Jessica didn't know what to say. Life isn't always fair, she thought, but it did no one any good to tell them that. If they didn't know it already the words were meaningless. So she simply said, "You need rest, too, Mrs. Sanderson. He'll need you at your best. Why don't you try to sleep?"

"Oh, I couldn't, I'd never be able to close my eyes, thinking about that poor man tied to the wheel of the stage. And Fred . . ." She moaned again.

"Try," the younger woman said patiently. "Close your eyes. I'll be awake for a while if Mr. Sanderson needs anything."

"He's not used to this sort of thing," Mildred murmured after a moment. "Fred never liked shooting at or killing anything, not even a rabbit, not even in the war." Her voice trailed off, and Jessica thought she was going to continue the thought. But the tired woman's eyelids drooped, and after a moment her breathing became deep and regular, broken once or twice by a catch, then resuming the rhythm of sleep.

Jessica Allen rose quietly and returned to the main room of the station, carefully closing the door to the sleeping room.

It was an uneasy time of waiting. There was bad feeling in the station, particularly toward its owner, Art Cheever. At one point, when someone repeated the inevitable question, "Do you think they'll be back?", the man called Rimmer said, "I ain't losin' my scalp to save someone's been tradin' with them savages. If they want any hair, Cheever, we'll just have to give 'em yours."

The cold-blooded suggestion produced a shocked silence. There was no protest, not even from Cheever, who supplied a sickly grin as if to suggest that he knew Rimmer was joking.

As the evening wore on Jessica Allen sensed something subtly different about Rimmer and about the others' attitude toward him. They attended him with a kind of obeisance, eager to be part of any conversation he joined, ready to drink with him, quick to follow his orders about trussing up the marshal's killer, Blaine, readily acquiescing to Rimmer's recommendations about having two men on the night watch.

And ready, Jessica wondered, to turn on Art Cheever if that was what Rimmer decided?

It did not take her long to realize that the other men in the room—Cheever, Chandler, Adams, the wounded Sanderson, young Noah Calder—were afraid of Rimmer. They had been afraid of him ever since the discovery of the marshal's murder in the stables, when Rimmer had dragged the half-conscious killer before them and viciously kicked him in the head.

The change in Rimmer himself was subtler, more difficult for her to pinpoint. For some reason he made her think of an adolescent boy who had just had his first woman. There was a more visible arrogance about him, a cocksureness, an air of command, even a hint of contempt for the others who crowded around him so eagerly. Maybe these things had always been there, she thought, but not so openly displayed. The marshal had checked him a little, she supposed. And with Holifield dead, and Cullom Blaine helpless, there was no one to . . .

What? Stand up to him? Stop him from . . . what?

Restless with these thoughts, Jessica moved over to the cot where Sanderson lay. He was, in fact, sleeping, though not at all peacefully, the pain showing sometimes in his face even as he slept. He would need a doctor to look at his shoulder, she thought. And he would have a hard, painful journey to get to one.

She sat on the wooden chair beside the cot and leaned back, grateful for a chance to rest her feet. After a mo-

ment her glance strayed across the room toward Cullom
Blaine. He didn't look like much of a catamount now,
bruised and battered as he was, tied hand and foot. His
worn range clothes were dirty now from being dragged
across the floor of the stables. His sandy hair was dark and
matted where he had bled from the blow to his head. One
side of his face was bruised and swollen, turning shades of
purple—Jessica had seen Rimmer's kick, an act of casual
violence that had sickened her in spite of the revulsion
she felt for what Blaine had done. She also saw something
she hadn't noticed before, perhaps because it was usually
hidden by Blaine's hat. It was an angry red patch high on
his forehead, about the size of a silver dollar, like the mark
of a deep burn where the skin healed over but was never
afterward the same.

A burn, she thought. What had caused it? But that was
probably a foolish question about such a man.

She leaned her head back against the rough texture of
the stone wall, closing her eyes. In the darkness she heard
the low mutter of the men talking across the room. But
the face in the darkness of her shuttered eyes was
Blaine's . . .

On the one hand she despised Blaine for what he had
done to the marshal. He was typical of the lawless, brutal,
senseless violence so often found on this frontier. He was a
hard, angry man, and it showed. There was nothing gentle about him. And yet . . . something in the picture was
awry. The way he talked to young Charity Calder. The
way he looked at Jessica herself at times. There was a
quiet strength and decency in him that was at odds with
the surface picture.

Jessica shook off the impression. The marshal was dead,
murdered, shot in the back. No one had believed Blaine's
curt denial of guilt. Who else had reason to kill Holifield?

Only Rimmer was there in the stables with them, and the marshal had not threatened him. Blaine was his prisoner, scheduled to be taken for trial—hanged if the marshal's opinion was correct. Blaine had every reason to act to save his neck.

Voices rose, causing her to open her eyes.

"What's Navaja after? You know more'n you're tellin', Cheever." It was Rimmer again, splashing whiskey into a glass as he glared at Cheever.

"I don't know what you're talkin' about."

"You know damned well. What's he want with you? Did you cheat him some way, Cheever? Wouldn't put it past you. By God, we can fix that. We can put you out there, tie you to one of them wheels on the stage where he can see you, and maybe he'll be satisfied with that."

The words produced an uneasy silence, the other men exchanging glances, their eyes avoiding Rimmer, who grinned nastily and swallowed whiskey. He was acting the bully, Jessica thought with a surprise of recognition. It was an act she knew well . . .

She veered away from the thought as if it threatened her. Her gaze drifted back to Blaine, but she was thinking now of her own plight. She would be glad to catch the eastbound stage at last if it came as scheduled. Glad to escape this territory. And yet . . . she did not feel about the rugged land as Mildred Sanderson did. Jessica found beauty in its sweep and its silences, its battering skies, its promise, if only the men upon the land could be tamed. She would miss it. And what did she have to go back to? Her own family was gone, the friends she had known in recent years were scattered across the country, for she had been an army vagabond, like her husband.

And at last she sighed and let the thoughts come. It was

Joe she had been thinking of when she saw Rimmer acting the bully. Sergeant Joseph Allen, her late husband.

"I'm no angel," Joe Allen would say of himself, making it a kind of boast. Among the men of the 4th Cavalry he was known as garrulous but quick-tempered, and a heavy drinker. Twice he had been broken in rank from sergeant, but each time he eventually won his stripes back. A good soldier, everyone said. Can raise hell off duty, but count on him when the bugle calls.

Jessica Allen knew those things about her husband, and other things that took place only behind the scenes, a wife's private knowledge. Like the way Joe liked to slap her around when he'd been drinking. Just to keep her alert, he had said one time, laughing. And to keep her in her place. Those moments were hints of the violence in him that was quick to erupt.

Joe enjoyed fighting. He loved the Indian campaigns, but he also relished a fight any chance that came. Whenever he went to a town she was a little afraid of what might happen, because there had been many fights. Of course, the soldiers fought in camp sometimes, too. Joe said you couldn't crowd men together like that without having some friction, or even the simple need to let off steam once in a while. And if a sergeant couldn't whip any man who served under him, Joe would say, they would never respect him. It was, Jessica thought, a narrow, mean view of soldiering.

Joe Allen was a violent man, but not a killer. Mostly he fought with his fists, rarely with a knife, never with guns. Guns, he had said once, were for killing Indians and Rebs.

But not everyone chose the same weapons. Joe Allen had been in town with some men of his detachment, several old-timers like himself, hard-drinking men. But there were hard men in the town as well, the gamblers and tradesmen and hangers-on in a settlement that existed mainly because of the nearby military post. Allen liked to gamble, and it was something he did badly when he was drinking. He was a reckless card player, a plunger, and as he drank he lost some of his alertness and cunning.

Jessica Allen knew only what they told her about that last night. "Joe was drinkin' some, sure," Corporal Rademacher told her, not meeting her eyes. "We all was, but we none of us was what you'd call drunk. You know how the old Sarge was, he could carry a bigger load than most men can swallow. Anyways, somethin' happened at that table. Sergeant Allen started yellin' at this cardsharp, a kind of dude he was, fancy clothes and suspenders and all, a wispy kind of man you wouldn't look at twice he didn't have all that finery, like a goddam peacock. First thing we knew was the Sarge standin' up, accusin' the gambler of cheatin' him. Said he wanted to see what the feller had up his sleeves. Well, everythin' went kind of quiet then, that whole saloon shut up, and the Sarge blinked some, as if he knew he'd got himself backed into a corner and wasn't sure how he'd got there. But you know Sergeant Allen, ma'am, he never backed off from no fight. Private Sedgewick and me, we tried to get to him, but there was a bunch of them townies in the saloon and they crowded us back, warnin' us to stay out of it. They had guns and all. Anyways, the Sarge did his own fightin', nobody had to do it for him. That's what we told ourselves." Young Corporal Rademacher's watery eyes peered at her as if to see what kind of accusation he might find in hers, but they swam away quickly. "We should've been with him," he muttered.

"No one's blaming you, Corporal," Jessica said, thinking that it was expected of her.

Rademacher plunged ahead with relief, wanting to

wind up the sad tale, wanting to be away from the griev-
ing widow. "Sarge didn't pull his gun on the dude. He
wanted him to fight, is all. Sarge wanted to see what he
had up his sleeves, and if the dude wouldn't show him
then Sarge was gonna tear them sleeves right off'n him."
Rademacher paused, licking his lips. *Tell it,* Jessica
thought numbly. *Go ahead, tell it!* "It happened so sudden, you could see the surprise on Sergeant Allen's face.
The gambler, he had a little hideout gun up his sleeve.
Maybe he had some cards there, too, but he just dropped
his arm and that little derringer popped into his hand, and
when Sarge grabbed at him across the table, upsettin' the
cards and a bottle and tippin' over one of the chairs, that
derringer jumped into the dude's hand and it went off
with a little bang, like it was a toy gun. And the Sarge just
looked kinda surprised, as if he couldn't believe it was
happenin'. And he just sat down, holdin' his chest . . ."

Jessica Allen knew most of the rest of it. How the angry
soldiers had been hustled out of town, back to the fort.
How a detachment returned later, led by two officers, to
talk to the sheriff. And how the whole town appeared to
back up the story that the soldier had provoked a fight,
accusing a man of cheating and then attacking him in a
drunken rage. The town lived off the men of the fort,
enjoyed their protection, but disliked them at the same
time. And the sheriff said there was nothing that could be
done. Some of the soldiers at Fort Tracy talked of taking
matters into their own hands, but before that talk could
lead to anything word came that the gambler had left
town.

And that was the end of it.

The end, too, of a part of Jessica Allen's life. She had
married young, with a romantic girl's view of what a soldier was, and Joe Allen with his dark curly hair and his

grin and his Irish eyes—and even, she thought reluctantly, that hint of unruly wildness in him—had left her a little dizzy with wanting him.

The way of life marriage had purchased for Joe Allen's wife was no bed of roses. Nor was the life of any soldier's wife in the Army of the West an easy one. They had moved often, and often Joe was away for long periods of time. She would feel like something put away on a shelf while he went on about the real business of life, the soldiering and fighting. And then he would be back and there would be a period of activity and excitement and planning, and sometimes of tedium and boredom. And then they would be moving again, or he would be in the field again and she would go back on the shelf . . .

Jessica was not sure, now, if she had been happy. At first, certainly, she had thought she was, with the blind happiness of a young bride. But she couldn't quite remember how long that had lasted. There had been a continuing pride, both in him and what he was doing, for she was proud of being an army wife. But she thought of Joe now not with longing but with an odd sadness, as if she pitied him, mourning not the man but the waste of all that reckless courage and zest for living. She wondered when the love had died.

Now there was sadness, emptiness, a feeling of hatred and contempt for the man who had killed him. It didn't seem enough for all the years, the best years of a woman's life . . .

Her eyes met those of Cullom Blaine. Cold gray eyes, she thought, eyes without pity or compassion. The eyes of an outlaw, a murderer, like the man who had killed Joe Allen.

Eyes that, meeting hers, seemed to flare with unexpected anger.

Jessica looked away, disconcerted, surprised by the intensity of her own reaction.

11

Cullom Blaine felt the weight of the widow's gaze and looked away in anger. Not with her but with himself. Anger because he had been stirred by her. Anger because he had looked at her as a woman. Anger because, for a moment earlier on, when she had bent solicitously over the wounded Sanderson, the sight had merged with another image, so deeply buried in Blaine's memory that he had felt a physical shock at the clarity of it when it suddenly surfaced.

Most times it was harder for him to remember Samantha clearly now, he acknowledged with a mixture of regret and sadness and bitter resignation. But every once in a while a sharp detail would poke out of his memory like a branch projecting into the open from the depths of a dark pool. The flash of Sam's teeth, which were large and prominent. The snap of humorous challenge in her eyes. The way she moved about the kitchen of the Texas house, her generous hips brushing against the side of a table or chair. The way her dark brown hair spilled over her shoulders when she let it down at night . . .

Blaine shook himself, the anger still in him. Yet he did not shy away from the memories, as he had once done, unable to cope with them. Mostly he welcomed them now, because they had become more rare, and less clear. Not welcoming them seemed a kind of betrayal.

Cullom Blaine had to stop and think how many years it

had been. Too many. The force that had pushed him along his solitary trail was still there. It would remain there as long as even one of the men he hunted was still alive, the men who had boarded her inside the house and set it afire. But the rage was not as all-consuming as it had once been. Blaine supposed it was not possible to be driven that hard without letup, year after year. Something had to give, either the man or the passion.

He was not certain, aside from that chance pose of neck and shoulders and tilted head, what it was about Jessica Allen that reminded him of Samantha. Not physical appearance, for the two women were not that much alike. Perhaps nothing more than the gentleness when she spoke to Sanderson and his wife. Perhaps the quiet that came over her face at times when she didn't know she was being watched. Perhaps the hint of sadness in her eyes, a suggestion of lost magic, which had never completely left Samantha's eyes after she lost their first child at birth.

She was four months pregnant when she died.

Blaine gave a convulsive wrench against the rawhide that bound him, heaving with all his strength, the blood pounding in his temples. At last he fell back, spent, and was still, letting the sudden spurt of frustration drain away. So the passion was still there, he thought. All he had to do was open the door and let it out.

He would see two of Samantha's killers soon, at long last. Tom and Art Clancy. But if they came and found him trussed up as he was, the boys and Rimmer would do a dance around his corpse . . .

Blaine heard shuffling steps, a clatter of something knocked aside, and Rimmer's face loomed over him. "Ain't no use, Blaine. You're hog-tied for sure. But you go right on tryin' to bust loose." Rimmer's nasty grin was lopsided, his breath strong enough to cure the sick. He'd been drinking heavily all evening, and Blaine wondered with a faint tug of hope how much longer it would be before the bottle bedded him down. As if sensing his thought Rimmer said, "I'll be watchin'. Hell, I'd jest as soon cut you loose myself so's I could gut-shoot you and watch you curl up. But it don't matter to me much whichever way. If the Clancy boys does it, I get to watch."

He grinned again, swaying over Blaine. When there was no response he waved one hand airily, turned and staggered off.

As Rimmer returned to the bar, Cullom Blaine noticed young Noah Calder staring after him, his eyes registering the shock brought by Rimmer's mocking taunt.

It was in that moment that the faint hope awakened in Blaine by Rimmer's drunkenness began to take a more visible shape.

The two riders picked their way among huge rocks broken and tumbled by some ancient upheaval of the earth. Neither man had spoken in a long time when one of the horses staggered on loose shale and had to be reined up hard to prevent a fall. "Goddam it, Art!" one of the men swore. "If this horse breaks a leg I'll break one of yours, see how you like it."

"Whyn't you blow a trumpet, let everyone know we're here?"

"We can't keep goin' when it's this dark." Under the lowering sky it was black as pitch among the rocks. When the horses emerged onto a clear slope the grumbling rider let out an explosive sigh of relief. Even in the open it was still dark on this overcast night, but at least you could see your horse's ears prick.

"Apaches hate the dark worse'n you do," Art Clancy said.

"If'n that's so, why do you care about me makin' noise?"

Art turned in the saddle to glare at his brother. "You gonna argue about every little thing?"

Tom Clancy relapsed into a sullen silence. The horses wound carefully down the grade until it leveled off. Ahead there was a notch formed by two huge rock formations, the trail cutting through the bottom of the V. The purple night sky, lighter than the dark of solid objects at ground level, was framed by the slanting walls. In single file the two riders rode toward the notch, the steady clop of hoofs the only sound in the night's stillness.

Tom's resentment of his older brother never lasted long —Art had always been the leader of the pair—and after a few minutes he kneed his roan just enough to bring him up beside Art. Speaking in a low tone he said, "You reckon Rimmer'll be at Cheever's Station by now?"

"Should be."

"Blaine's still ahead of us."

"Not far ahead."

"Sumbitch is gonna get his," Tom said. He was half hoping that Rimmer would have caught up to Blaine before he and his brother did, but that was only because of a grudging respect for Cullom Blaine. Who'd ever have thought Blaine could go against Abe Stillwell and come away standing, or even against Seevers and Keatch and Brownie Hayes? He was crazy, that's what he was. Indians were afraid of crazy folks, and maybe they had the right of it. You couldn't tell what such a man might do.

But if Rimmer got to Blaine first, the Clancy brothers would have to pay up. They'd agreed on it, at a time when they were especially uneasy after learning of Ned Keatch's death; but now it seemed like a hell of a price to pay.

"You figger Rimmer's worth what we're payin' him?"

"We ain't payin' him nothin' unless he puts Blaine down, one way or another."

"Yeah, but . . ."

"You still complainin' about your money? Damn it, Tom, whose money was it, anyways? It's Blaine's own gold, for Chrissakes! It ain't like it's somethin' you earned with your own sweat."

Tom Clancy turned sullen again. He'd earned that money, his share of it. Paid for it with three years in Huntsville. Granted, they had found the money in Blaine's house. The woman never told where it was, they'd just found it on their own, prying up some boards Wes Hannifan said had a hollow sound when you walked across them. The cache had been disappointing—apparently Blaine didn't keep much of his money hidden in the house at all, in spite of the rumors that had brought the gang there in Blaine's absence. It was said that he didn't trust banks and had the earnings from two summers stored away, the results of his most successful cattle drives. But what the gang of robbers had found was a small stake, penny ante when it had to be split up eight ways.

It was partly because of their angry frustration over the small findings that they had worked the woman over the way they did. That, and Hannifan saying that she knew who they were and could identify them to Blaine and the law. They'd had no choice, really. They'd done what they had to do.

Tom dropped back as they neared the notch and the trail narrowed. They rode through it single file, and as they reached the end of it the land fell away suddenly and Art grunted softly. Tom could barely make out Art's hand, abruptly gesturing him to halt.

Tom could feel his heart hammering. "Jesus, Art, what is it?" he whispered. "Apaches? That bastard Navaja?"

For a moment Art Clancy didn't answer. Then he gave another grunt. "It's a camp, right enough, but not 'paches. Damned if I don't . . ." He broke off, and looking past his shoulder at that moment Tom saw the faint glow of a campfire at the base of some cliffs. He saw the flash of Art's teeth and was surprised to realize Art was grinning. "Soldiers!" Art said. "It's your lucky night after all, Tom. It's the cavalry!"

They approached the camp slowly, making plenty of noise to warn the sentries. When they were close enough to the campfire to be clearly visible a sharp command stopped them. "Halt! Now come in slow and easy . . . that'll do it."

A uniformed sentry, rifle at the ready, stepped out of the shadows to examine the two riders. Visibly relaxing, he waved them on in.

The detachment was led by a self-assured young officer named Arnold Wilson, a lieutenant. Not long out of West Point, Art Clancy guessed, though he was shrewd enough not to let his dislike of officers show. Wilson had led his patrol in a wide sweep across the plains south of the Guadalupes, following his orders "to observe the presence of any hostiles in the area, and to report back to Command any such activity, but under no circumstances to engage the enemy in hostile action unless attacked."

"You run onto any 'paches?" Art Clancy asked.

Wilson shook his head. The sweep had proved uneventful. Five days in the saddle, his troopers were eager to return to Fort Tracy. And, in fact, the patrol was heading south in the morning, which probably accounted, Art thought, for the relaxed mood of the camp, many of the soldiers joking, playing cards, or engaged in raucous debate.

"We seen some smoke," Art said. "Yesterday early it was. Indian smoke, I mean."

There had been smoke sighted, climbing above the hills to the northwest, Lieutenant Wilson agreed, but no one could say who had sent up the signals or what they meant. If indeed they meant anything at all. "If you have seen any hostiles, sir, you have the advantage of us."

Art Clancy asked the question uppermost in his mind. "Did you get as far west as Cheever's Station? We was headin' that way." Art chuckled with false joviality. "We wouldn't much like to lock horns with that Apache renegade if he's out."

"Do you mean Navaja, sir?" Wilson asked with a trace of asperity. When would these settlers stop worrying over every wild rumor? If Navaja could be in every place he was rumored to be, and leaving the bloody carnage in his wake that was chronicled in those same fearful stories, he would deserve his reputation as a scourge of the plains. "Don't place too much stock in the stories you hear about him. We were at Cheever's Station night before last." Wilson smiled. "The only Indian in sight was Cheever's squaw."

Art and Tom Clancy exchanged quick glances. "Was the westbound stage in yet, when you was there?" Art asked.

"No, but we've had no reports of troubles with the stage," the lieutenant said. "I can assure you, if you're heading for the station, you'll find it peaceful there."

Tom Clancy grinned suddenly, his relief plain to see, and Art himself had to rein in an impulse to laugh. "We'll be ridin' over that way in the mornin', then," Art said.

"You're welcome to our campfire," the officer said after a brief hesitation. He didn't much like the look of the pair, but civility overrode his misgivings. After all, what harm could they do?

12

In the early hours of the morning Cheever's Station was deceptively peaceful. Outside the station it remained dark, and within there was only a single lamp glowing near the bar. No one moved about. A short while ago there was a change in sentinel duty, Noah Calder along with Chandler the drummer taking over for Art Cheever and Clay Adams. Cheever had disappeared abruptly into his back bedroom, while Adams, judging by the snores coming from a corner of the main room, had fallen instantly to sleep. The drummer had drunk heavily during the evening and he had not stirred in some time. He remained at his post near the front door to the station, his slumped posture suggesting that, though he was supposed to be keeping watch with Noah, he too had fallen asleep.

Noah Calder crouched beside Blaine. "What's going to happen, friend?"

Blaine regarded him in silence for a moment. "The Apaches will be back. Probably in the morning."

"How can thee be so sure? The others . . . I mean, they all seem to think it's over."

"They're not thinking, they're wishing. That's Navaja out there, with a bunch of hotheaded young warriors. He's called them together for this, and he's not going to turn and slink off now like a whipped dog. If he did, they wouldn't follow him again. They wouldn't believe in his medicine."

"His medicine?" Noah looked puzzled.

"Indians believe in medicine. Not the kind you swallow. More like . . . a power you have, so that nothing can hurt you or stop you. Not even a white man's bullet."

Noah said nothing for a while. His gaze wandered the room, shifting slowly from one figure to another. Someone slipped out the back door but Blaine was not in a position to see who it was. Noah was staring at Rimmer, who had dropped off long ago, slipping into what was more a whiskey-sodden stupor than sleep. "What will happen to you, Mr. Blaine?"

Blaine smiled faintly in the darkness. "You'd have to ask him. But I reckon you have a good idea, son."

"Why did thee kill the marshal? Because he was going to take thee to trial?"

"I didn't shoot him," Blaine said curtly.

"But . . . if thee didn't . . ." Suddenly Noah Calder appeared startled, his gaze darting back across the room toward the unconscious Rimmer.

"He's a bounty hunter," Blaine said. "Some men have put a price on my head, and Rimmer aims to collect. He couldn't do that if the marshal had me in custody. From what he says, those men will be here soon. When they come . . ." His wide shoulders lifted in a shrug. "It might not matter much, with Navaja and his braves out there working up their courage."

"Can't we hold out? This station seems quite sturdy, and we seem to have plenty of guns and ammunition—" Noah caught himself, color showing in his cheeks even in the dim light as he was reminded that they were guns and ammunition he could not bring himself to use.

"They haven't tried to burn it yet," Blaine said quietly. "The walls will stand, but they could smoke us out."

Noah Calder stared at him. For the first time the full

implications of what Blaine was telling him seemed to take hold. It wasn't just a matter of holding off the Apaches for a little while longer until rescue came. There would be no rescue. The cavalry had come and gone; they had no reason to return soon. The Apache chief had committed himself and wouldn't give up. There was no way to escape—the Apaches would be able to steal the horses from the stables almost any time they wanted. One by one the defenders inside the station would be worn down, wounded or killed. Or, if the fighting went on too long, the Indians might decide to burn them out. The walls of the station were of adobe on three sides to a height of five feet—a tall man in his boots had to stoop if he moved close to the walls or went through a door—but the log-pole roof was vulnerable to fire, as were the doors and shutters. How long could the station hold out?

Noah Calder thought of Charity, and of the other women, and a chill trickled along his spine. He had heard tales of what the Apaches did to white women . . . Even if only half of what he had heard were true, the possibility was unthinkable.

"Dear God in heaven," Noah whispered. "What can be done?"

Blaine met his eyes in the dimness. "You can start by cutting me loose."

Jessica Allen had slept little, and that badly. On impulse she finally rose and slipped through the kitchen to the back door of the stables, surprised to find Cheever's Indian woman there rather than in their tiny bedroom. The woman, huddled on a wooden chair in a corner, said nothing, but her eyes were open as Jessica carefully opened the back door and stepped outside.

For a little while she stood motionless, hugging a shawl

around her shoulders against the chill of the night air. The low clouds which had blotted out the stars were breaking up to the west, and she could see a sprinkling of glitter here and there through gaps in the clouds.

But the hills, the canyons, the trees crowded along the banks of the stream, all were black, impenetrable. Jessica thought of the Apaches out there and shivered, taking an involuntary step backward toward the door. She glanced over her shoulder, reassuring herself that the door was open and only a few feet away.

The men all said that Apaches seldom if ever fought at night. She remembered Joe saying the same thing—his regiment had escaped an ambush and won a partial victory in a battle with the Indians because, he had said with some incredulity, the hostiles had withdrawn as soon as it was dark, allowing the soldiers to regroup. Jessica wondered if it was superstition, and the question made her realize how little she knew about the Apaches or, for that matter, any other Indians of the West.

She stared toward the deep shadows of the surrounding hills, wondering if the Apaches were out there now, regrouping in their own way, preparing for the next day's battle . . .

She shivered again. She ought to go inside. But she lingered a little longer, glad to be in the open, away from the close smells and smoke of the crowded station. They were wonderful skies, she thought, these western skies . . .

It had taken Blaine a while to convince young Noah Calder to do what he had wanted to do all along—take advantage of the fact that both Rimmer and the other night sentry, Ray Chandler, were asleep, and cut the rawhide bonds that held Blaine prisoner. And Blaine warned the young man bluntly of what his action meant. "You can't stay here, you have to understand that. If you cut me free, he'll know it"—a nod toward Rimmer—"and he'll kill you."

Noah paled. "He won't know . . ."

"He'll know. You're not the sort who can hide it." The honest sort, Blaine thought. "I wouldn't ask you to do it if you didn't face as much danger doing nothing." When he saw the hesitation in Noah's eyes, the renewed uncertainty, Blaine said, "Navaja is as much a threat as Rimmer. More of a threat to . . . to all the women here." Especially to your young wife, he thought, not wanting to say it.

Noah Calder was quick to take his meaning. He bit at his lower lip, his eyes worried. "But what can I do?"

"You can ride, can't you?"

"Yea, friend, I grew up with horses," Noah said. "But where would thee have me go? And what horse would I ride? Our horse was among those taken by the Indians."

"I'll get you a horse from the stables—my horse—and point you south. You just ride as fast as you can go, you don't stop for nothin' until you catch up with soldiers."

Noah stared at him uncertainly, for a moment at a loss as to what to say. The desire to help had been nagging at him all day. But as he thought of riding alone and unarmed through the hills where the Apaches waited, he remembered the wretched man the Apaches had tied to the wagon wheel and he was touched by fear. Besides, he reminded himself, his first duty was to protect Charity. He shook his head. "Nay, I cannot leave Charity here alone."

"She won't be alone," Blaine said, then stopped. He was asking Calder not only to put himself at great risk, a greenhorn attempting to bolt past the Apaches at night, but also to leave his wife, if not alone, at best in danger.

The knowledge awakened the buried guilt Blaine had felt in the restless hours of a thousand nights for leaving Samantha alone and unprotected. Could he ask someone else to take that kind of risk? But the decision had to be made. Guilt, if there was any, had to be accepted. "She won't be alone," he repeated. "I'll see to that. That's a promise, son. And if you cut me loose, Charity will be safer with you gone. Rimmer won't take it out on her, not with all the others watching and knowing. And if you can get to the cavalry, if you can find that Lieutenant Wilson who was here night before last when we come to the station . . . well, that's the one chance for everyone here to stay alive. If someone doesn't bring help, Navaja won't let up. He's after something, or someone."

But in the end it wasn't Noah Calder who made the hard decision. It was Charity. Noah insisted he had to tell her—he couldn't leave her alone without her knowing what he was doing. From a distance Blaine watched their whispered conference—Noah brought her out of the communal sleeping room and drew her over to one side of the main room, away from the others—and saw the young woman glance his way while they talked in urgent whispers. Would she object to having Noah set him free, even if it didn't create a threat from Rimmer? Did she, like the others, believe him guilty of the marshal's murder? Blaine realized that he was asking a lot of a young woman thrust into a situation unlike any she had ever known, facing dangers she could only imagine, asking her to trust someone she did not even know who was said to be a wanted man, a murderer. But he remembered the way she had reacted after the Apaches who had been circling the little wagon had been driven off, her remarkable self-composure and quiet determination, and he drew hope from that.

Noah Calder hurried across the room toward him, glancing in Rimmer's direction anxiously before he squatted at Blaine's side. "We'd best do it now," Noah said, the tension along with his unspoken fear making his voice tremble slightly. "That's what Charity says. We'd best hurry, before Rimmer wakes up. And before it's light and the Apaches come back!"

13

Cautiously, working in dim light with a stubby pock-
etknife, conscious of the rasp of his own quick breathing,
Noah Calder sawed at the strips of rawhide that tied Cullom Blaine's hands and feet. Noah kept glancing in the
direction of the sleeping Rimmer, his heart leaping every
time there was a rustle of clothing or a change in the
timbre of a snore.

Blaine rubbed his wrists and flexed his fingers, trying to
bring life back to his hands. But as he rose to his knees
from his sitting position on the floor, Rimmer spoke. Both
Blaine and Noah Calder froze. Then Rimmer rolled over,
pawing at his face once before he settled down again.
Blaine let out his breath slowly. He had hardly begun to
relax when Rimmer turned again in his sleep and muttered something. He was close to waking, Blaine guessed.

There was no time to look for a weapon. Beckoning
Noah after him, Blaine slipped toward the back of the
main room. Passing Charity Calder he paused briefly,
their eyes holding. Blaine nodded, lacking words to ex-
press what he felt, then hurried past her into the darkness
of the kitchen.

He was instantly aware of Cheever's Woman watching
him. They stared at each other in silence. The Indian did
not move or make any outcry. Blaine was fairly sure she
wouldn't. Her loyalty was to Cheever, not to Rimmer or

any of the others. And she would not have missed Rimmer's threat to Cheever.

Once in the open Blaine ran toward the stables, Noah Calder close behind him. It took Blaine only a moment, even in the darkness, to find his buckskin in one of the stalls on his right, where he had seen the horse earlier that night. The horse nickered his pleasure as Blaine led him out of the stables. The buckskin was fresh, rested, eager, and he nuzzled Blaine playfully while stamping his hoofs. "Hold him," Blaine said to Noah Calder. "Can you ride in that?" he added, nodding at Noah's long gray coat.

"I can manage, if I leave it unbuttoned."

Blaine found his saddle and blankets in a corner of the stall. While he saddled the horse, working quickly, he noted that Calder seemed comfortable enough with the buckskin. "He'll run hard when you get into the open. There's no Indian pony will catch him once you get clear."

"I used to race some," Noah said, with the reluctant tone of a confession. "That was before I joined the community."

He meant the Shakers, Blaine understood. Was horse racing banned among them? Considered sinful? He supposed it was, for racing horses was almost always accompanied by gambling. Blaine regarded the young man thoughtfully for a moment, then turned a hard, quartering gaze toward the surrounding hills. "The danger will be getting the first jump. The Apaches might have pulled back for the night, but they could have a scout posted. You have to know there's a risk, especially . . ."

"Yea, friend, I know," Noah said. The risk was increased because he wouldn't shoot back or even carry a gun. "But as thee has said, there is as much risk in doing nothing."

As if reminded that he also was without a weapon,

Blaine dug a knife in its sheath from his saddlebag and stuffed it under his belt. "Go now while you can," Blaine said. "Walk him over thataway. When you get beyond the rise, hit the leather and ride!"

Noah Calder nodded, swallowed a lump of anxiety, and glanced back toward the station, where Charity was visible in the kitchen doorway, one hand at her throat. "Good luck, friend," Noah whispered to Blaine.

He left quickly, leading the buckskin as Blaine had directed toward a dip between two hills to the south. For a moment Blaine lost him in shadows on the slope. Then he picked up the shapes of both Noah and the horse as they were briefly outlined against the night sky at the top of the rise.

Abruptly Blaine turned toward Cheever's Station. Rimmer might awake at any moment. When he did, and found Blaine gone, the gunman would come after him.

Charity Calder had disappeared inside, closing the door behind her, probably as soon as Noah had vanished from sight over the hill. The fact that there was no time to dwell on either sympathy or gratitude did not lessen what Blaine felt toward the young Shaker couple. He would not forget what they had done—nor could he forget the pledge he had made to Noah about Charity's safety.

The night was empty of sound or movement. But not really empty, Blaine knew. Would Noah Calder get through? Had he sent the young man to his death to save his own skin? Blaine shook off the question. He was an old hand at assessing the repercussions of his actions. A choice had had to be made, and brooding over it changed nothing.

As he took a step toward the station he saw a flash of movement, white at the corner of his eye, and went into a running crouch. The shape leaped also, swiftly like an animal panicked, but not toward Blaine—toward the back door that led into the kitchen. The white flutter of cloth took shape, the skirts of a garment of some sort visible beneath a long coat, and in the instant that Blaine understood what he had seen he also recognized the danger— not the threat of an Indian striking at him out of darkness but the equally real hazard of someone warning Rimmer that his captive had escaped.

Blaine caught the woman's arm as she reached for the door. He pulled her away from the doorway. As her eyes widened and she started to cry out he clamped one hand over her mouth.

For a moment they stared at each other, the shock in Jessica Allen's eyes reflecting his own surprise. Then he heard a mutter of voices from inside the station. "Sorry," he said. "I can't let you say what you've seen."

His right fist traveled no more than a foot. It struck her on the side of the jaw, snapping her head back. Blaine caught her as her knees buckled and she slumped forward. Lifting her easily in his arms, he carried her limp form away from the station toward the shadowed hills.

Another pair of eyes, sharp as a hawk's, watching from a distant promontory, saw the figures of a horse and rider dip over the hill behind Cheever's Station and heard the sudden rush of hoofs as the rider headed south.

Navaja's mouth, a lipless slash in the hard bronzed face, tightened as he considered. Even at this distance, and in the dark, he thought he recognized the horse, though he could not identify the rider. Navaja had an appreciation for horses, and the buckskin was a noble animal. But what caused him to hesitate was his memory of the man who rode that horse. The man who had spared the Apache chief's prize pony—if not Navaja's own life—in their brief encounter two suns before.

It required little insight to understand that the rider was heading in the direction of the army fort. But it was a punishing day's ride to the south at best. Even starting now the rider would be lucky to reach his destination before nightfall. The buckskin might survive such a ride, Navaja thought, but he could not make it shorter. And on his journey the rider would have to run a gauntlet of Apache warriors, some of whom were following the small detachment of pony soldiers.

All of which meant that letting the rider go presented little risk. Navaja's scouting report the previous day had confirmed that the cavalry patrol was now moving south, having apparently completed its own scouting mission. Even if the rider should overtake the soldiers and cause them to change course, Navaja would have ample warning. And if the rider chased the troopers all the way to the fort, it would be at least two suns before they would return.

All this went through the Apache's mind in a few seconds, time enough for him to weigh the circumstances and measure them against what the coming day would hold, and to make his decision. "Go then," Navaja said softly. "We are even, my horse-loving friend. When we meet again there will be no debt on either side." His hand moved absently to the heavy-bladed knife strapped to the side of his right leg. "Then we will meet as warriors."

His gaze swung to brood downward from his high vantage point toward the huddled shape of Cheever's Station in the distance, feeling a return of the bitter rage that was like fire in his belly. "This day is for another," he said aloud. "On this day there will be blood for blood."

Jessica Allen awakened slowly. When she tried to lift her head she gasped aloud at the pain that lanced her jaw. Bewildered, she put a hand to her face, lightly tracing with her fingertips the swollen cheek, the puffed lower lip.

Her eyes and her memory focused in the same instant. She glared up at Cullom Blaine. "You—!" His hand clamped over her mouth, muffling her cry.

"There are Apaches in these hills," he said softly. "Do you want to bring them to us?"

Her eyes went from anger to awareness, but the hostility remained in them. This part of the canyon was in deep shadow, but her eyes seemed to catch all the light there was. They glowed like two small fires.

"Are you going to keep quiet? It won't do you any good to yell at the station. Chances are no one will hear you, and if they do they won't come out in the dark. But it'll damn sure tell the Apaches where we are."

Finally she nodded. Blaine eased back to give her more room. A curve of rock wall close behind prevented him from straightening up or lifting his head. He watched the woman closely. He saw her look round, trying to place where they were, her mind beginning to assess her situation. Blaine felt a flicker of admiration for her coolness.

They were resting on a narrow ledge partway up the eastern wall of the ravine to the north of Cheever's Station, on the far side of the wagon road. When he left the station, carrying the unconscious woman, Blaine's first goal was the streambed that ran behind the stables and the pole corral. The cottonwoods and brush along its banks promised good cover. Almost immediately he recognized the utility of that same cover to the Apaches. He knew he could not shelter there safely for long. Instead he moved into the stream and followed it west of the station, where it crossed the wagon road and dipped into the blackness of the canyon beyond.

The lush growth on the floor of the canyon did not tempt him. Momentarily he left the woman propped in a niche between two large boulders while he climbed partway up the east wall, which, cut off from the rising sun, would hold the darkness longer. He was not sure exactly what he was looking for until he found it: a horizontal notch in the wall like the cleft of an ax, where rock arched over a narrow shelf. The shelf even angled inward at a slight decline, making it more invisible from below, and scraggly brush along its lip helped to screen it. If an Apache discovered the hiding place and tried to reach them from below, climbing, Blaine would hear him. And the wall of the canyon above the notch was relatively steep. An Indian could climb down the face easily, but not without dislodging dust and bits of crumbling rock. Though if anyone could, Blaine thought, it would be an Apache.

All in all, it seemed the best hole he could find to crawl into. He went back down to the floor of the canyon, picked up the unconscious woman, and returned to the shelf, climbing more carefully this time with his burden, pausing several times to listen to the silence of the canyon.

Fully awake now, Jessica Allen shifted toward the back of the narrow ledge as far as she could. There was not enough room for her to sit up, and she was acutely mindful of her closeness to Cullom Blaine in the confined space. She could not move without brushing against him.

As she felt her aching jaw once more, resentment flared, but it lacked real fire. Grudgingly she recognized that Blaine had done what he had to, according to his lights, when he had caught her outside the station. Obviously he was escaping. Just as obviously she would have cried out, giving the alarm, if she'd had the chance.

And she could have fared far worse. He might have left her anywhere, abandoning her to her own fate once he was clear of the station. She couldn't hold back the question. "Why didn't you just leave me back there? I couldn't have told anyone where you went."

Though Cullom Blaine looked at her, in the darkness she could see little of his expression. "There are Apaches all around the station. You think I'd leave you on the ground for them to find?"

The chilling words did more than remind her of the Indian threat. They also rekindled the puzzle of the man. Why would a killer care about her welfare? Surely she was a burden to him, an additional risk. And that raised another question. Why had he sent Noah Calder off on his horse instead of escaping himself?

"How can you be so sure the Apaches are still here?"

"They are," Blaine said.

"That's infuriating! You're not even answering me!"

"Keep your voice down," Blaine said quietly. "If I didn't know they aren't real close to us I'd have to shut you up again." He said it in a conversational tone, without emphasis, but she believed him.

Lowering her voice to a whisper she said, "How do you know they aren't close, then?"

"Because if they were we'd both be dead."

That silenced her for some time. She lay back against the rock shelf, unable to get as far from him as she would have liked. She was, in fact, decidedly sensitive to the warmth of his body. Finally she said, "I don't understand you."

"It's not something you have to do."

The words cut her off, as if he were erecting a barrier

between them. He turned in the narrow space, craning his neck to look upward into the darkness, and his thigh pressed against hers. The touch made her long for a real barrier.

"You're a murderer," she said.

"That's the way some folks look at it."

"Marshal Holifield did."

"The marshal had his own view of the law."

"And you killed him for it."

Blaine turned his head to stare at her for a long moment. "You talk too much."

"You shot him in the back!" she accused.

"I don't shoot people in the back," Blaine said, his tone disgusted.

"Well, if you didn't . . ." Jessica Allen stopped talking abruptly, startled—as Noah Calder had been earlier—by the persuasiveness of the other possibility. Blaine might very well *not* be the kind of man who would shoot someone in the back. Whatever else he might be, she would almost certainly have said he wasn't that. But would she say the same about Rimmer?

No, she thought, staring at Blaine's shadowed face. Rimmer was the one you wouldn't turn your back on.

"They say you're a hunter," she said after a moment. "A hunter of men."

"Do they?" He leaned out to survey the slope of the canyon wall below their niche. She wondered that he could see anything in the blackness. There were no sounds, no sign of life, only the thick shadows all around.

"Well, do you deny it?"

For a while she thought he wasn't going to answer. She felt his withdrawal, as if he had gone away somewhere without moving. But at last he spoke bluntly. "No."

"You're not a hunter?"

"No, I don't deny it. There are people I hunt."

Something in his tone caused her to persist, pursuing the point, trying to get past the barrier, as if, for reasons she did not yet comprehend, it were very important for her to understand. "Why?" she asked him. "What turned you into a killer?"

14

Rimmer was in a rage, and everyone at Cheever's Station was awake, shivering in the chill of this dark hour of the night—or with fear. His face was bright red, his eyes had a wildness in them. He paced back and forth across the main room like a caged animal, and the wild eyes lashed this way and that as if he were looking for something or someone to strike at. The others, after a few feeble questions that produced snarling eruptions of fury, were afraid to say anything to him at all. They waited, men and women, for his anger to abate.

They understood instinctively what they had no way of knowing from experience: that Rimmer's rages were dangerous. He could go out of control in an instant, and the two six-guns tied to his legs were the instruments with which he vented his anger—and without a second's thought. Once, in a saloon in Fort Worth, Rimmer had killed a man who had accidentally bumped his elbow when he lifted a glass. Rimmer's instant fury had so unnerved the other man that he'd made the mistake of trying to fight back, grabbing clumsily for his own gun. He had never dragged it clear of the leather before Rimmer poured five bullets in him, three from his right-hand gun and two from the left. There'd been a hue and cry, but witnesses bore out Rimmer's claim that the dead man had tried to draw on him.

This time his anger was compounded by a reluctance to

go after Blaine while it was still dark. He didn't believe Navaja and his braves were still in the hills around the station, but he couldn't be one hundred percent sure. The smidgen of doubt was enough to hold him back. Besides, darkness gave Blaine an advantage. Rimmer was afraid of no one man he could see. He was unwilling to go after a dangerous man—and he had no doubt that Blaine was such a man—without being able to see him.

As the storm within him began to spend itself, Rimmer returned to the unanswered questions. How had Blaine got loose? The rawhide strips that had bound him were missing. Rimmer knew that a strong man, given enough time to himself and sufficient determination, could stretch them. He should have checked and tightened the knots before going to sleep. Would have if he hadn't drunk so much and got careless. But was that what happened?

And what about the widow from Fort Tracy? What about the kid, the Easterner who wore that funny suit of clothes?

He turned to Charity Calder for that answer. She was sitting on the bench near the kitchen doorway, arms and shoulders hunched together as if she were cold. "Where is he?" Rimmer demanded. "Your husband, where'd he go?" The young woman would not look at him until he roughly tilted her face upward. "Run out on you, did he? With Blaine?"

When she still didn't answer, simply looking up at him, tight-lipped and resolute, he grabbed the front of her bodice and jerked her to her feet. Clay Adams protested, other voices rose, and Rimmer wheeled on them. His hot eyes speared Adams, singling him out. He thrust Charity back onto her bench seat against the wall and faced the young stage driver, his hands dangling loose over the twin six-guns. "You wanta answer for her? Damn you, I asked you a question!"

Adams shook his head, swallowing. He was a brave enough man in most situations, but the killing fury he saw in Rimmer's eyes took all the starch out of him. He knew that he was looking at death, that he would never be closer to it than he was in that moment. Adams shook his head again, a kind of jerk that wouldn't stop once he put it in motion. "No . . . uh, I never saw anything. I mean, I was asleep. I don't know what happened."

"Anyone else got somethin' to say? Anybody see anythin'? You—Chandler, ain't it?—you was supposed to be on guard, wasn't you?"

The drummer looked terrified. He started to shake and his voice shook as well. "I . . . uh . . . I didn't see a thing. That is, I . . . I guess I was asleep."

"Yeah, you were all asleep. Nobody saw a thing, nobody heard a thing. I oughta—" Rimmer saw a blur of movement out of the corner of his eye and whirled toward the kitchen. Cheever's squaw! "You!" he snarled. "Come outa there!"

The Indian woman shuffled silently out of the kitchen in her worn, blackened moccasins, her face as usual without expression. "You were awake, that right? In the kitchen?"

Woman stared at him with her black liquid eyes and said nothing. Cheever edged toward them, chewing his lower lip with nervous concern.

Suddenly Rimmer slapped her with the back of his hand. "You speak American, I know you do. Blaine and the kid, they went out through the kitchen, didn't they? You saw 'em go." Her eyes flicked toward Cheever and Rimmer spun toward the tall, round-shouldered station owner. "You got somethin' to put in the pot, Cheever?"

Cheever opened his mouth but nothing came out. He

licked his lips and tried again but the fear had dried up his protest.

Rimmer turned back to the Indian woman, calmly drew his left-hand gun, placed the muzzle against the side of her head, where the black hair looked as if it had been greased with lard, and cocked the hammer. "Tell her to answer me," he said to Cheever. "Tell her she talks or I pull this trigger and blow the top of her head off."

Rimmer ignored the small cries and choked-off protests from the others in the room. Cheever spoke quickly. "Do it!" he said to Woman. "Tell him everything you saw."

The still black pools of her eyes remained impenetrable, but she spoke quite clearly. "Young one take horse. Man who was tied go away on foot. He take woman with him."

"Why'd she go?" Rimmer demanded. "What was she doin' with him? Was she the one cut him loose?"

Woman shrugged. "She was outside. She would have returned. He catch her, carry her away."

"You mean she didn't want to go?"

Woman stared at him with contempt, as if the question answered itself.

"And Blaine didn't take off on his horse? It was the other one who rode away? The kid?"

Woman nodded. After a moment's hesitation, as if he regretted not having to punish her further, Rimmer holstered his weapon and shoved the squaw away. His attention swung back toward Charity Calder. "You heard what she said," he told the young Shaker woman. "So there ain't much point in you buttoning your lips like that. Your husband set Blaine free, I reckon."

"I don't know," she said.

"You don't know," he sneered, mimicking her. "You people lie just like the rest of us, huh? All that dancin' and caterwauling don't mean any more'n a snowflake in a blizzard. But maybe you don't mind tellin' us why he rode off."

"Mr. Calder is going to bring the cavalry back. Mr. Blaine is certain the Indians will attack us again. Unless we get help, he said, we will all be killed. Or . . ." Charity hesitated, her glance drifting toward Mildred Sanderson. "Or worse," she whispered.

"That's smoke!" Rimmer snapped. "They's finished, you could tell that yesterday the way they slacked off. They know they can't whip us, and they ain't so eager to die."

His anger cooling, Rimmer was beginning to assess the situation more clearly, considering the implications of what he had learned. Noah Calder had been sent south toward Fort Tracy. Even if he managed to get through safely, which seemed questionable—he hadn't looked like a man who could even hold on to the saddle—it was at least a day of hard riding to the fort. The army didn't exactly move in a hurry at the best of times. Even if they took Calder's warning seriously, they would still debate about it. And when the palavering was over and troops set off for Cheever's Station, there would be another full day's ride north. Two, three days all told. Plenty of time, in other words, for Rimmer to finish his business with Blaine.

But the Clancy brothers should get here a lot sooner than the cavalry. Rimmer had to make sure Blaine was his, dead or alive, before the Clancy boys arrived.

He went to one of the windows at the front of the station, opened the shutters and peered out. The night remained cloudy and dark. Should he go after Blaine anyway? Now?

Some things about Blaine puzzled him. Taking the woman with him, for instance. She would tie him down. Why not simply dump her? She couldn't mean anything to him, and it didn't make sense for a man like that to let himself be hobbled by a woman he didn't even know. Nor could Rimmer understand why Blaine had sent Calder off on his horse to summon help. Why not take it himself and light a shuck for parts unknown? He would have gained another long jump on Rimmer and the Clancy brothers.

Finally Rimmer shrugged off the questions. It was his good luck that Blaine hadn't run. He was nearby, Rimmer was certain of it. He was on foot and—

He turned again toward Woman, who regarded him in stoic silence. "Was he armed? Blaine? Did he grab a gun?"

She shook her head. Then her plump shoulders lifted in a shrug. She didn't know.

"If you're lyin' to me . . ."

"She doesn't know," Cheever said quickly. "But it's easy enough to check. If there are no guns missing, then he didn't have time to find one."

Rimmer wasn't sure the resulting search was any cast-iron certainty, but no weapons were missing. Even Blaine's own Walker Colt, heavy enough to make most men walk lopsided, was still safe behind the bar where Rimmer had put it himself.

Returning to the window he stared at the darkness, his thin lips twisting in an anticipatory smile.

Halfway up the east wall of the canyon Cullom Blaine lay flat on the narrow shelf, waiting for first light. He had surprised himself by responding to Jessica Allen's quiet question. What had turned him into a killer? And was that, in fact, what he was?

The words came out reluctantly at first, and they were spare, in the way of men like him throughout the West who didn't parade their feelings. "My wife Samantha was sick and I'd ridden into Martinsville for the doctor . . ."

Tom Wills, the doctor, had been late getting back to town, Blaine remembered, and he'd needed some sleep. They had set off before dawn, while it was still dark. The delay proved fatal. "I'd promised him breakfast when we got there. We saw the smoke when we was still a long ways off . . ." His tone was laconic, betraying nothing of the awakened anguish. "The robbers come while I was gone, lookin' for money. When they didn't find it they . . . they taken it out on her. After they'd done with her they set fire to the house while she was still inside, still alive . . ."

(He spilled out of the saddle, running too fast. Stumbled and sprawled onto his chest. He scrambled up. The heat of the flames seared his face and hands. The sound of them was a roar that filled his ears, blotting out everything else. He looked around wildly as he ran toward the house, refusing to believe that she could be trapped inside that hell's inferno. Then he heard her scream . . .)

"They'd boarded up the house, locked her inside. She couldn't get out. I could hear her . . . screaming."

(He ran toward the door, shouting. The roar of the flames drowned out his cries. He tore at the boards with his bare hands. The heat blistered his flesh, seared his eyes, blinding him. Tom Wills threw himself onto Blaine's back, trying to drag him away. Raging, Blaine threw his friend across the yard. He ripped the last boards away and rammed a boot heel against the door. It exploded inward. A solid blast of heat drove Blaine back against his will. The heat scorched his flesh and knifed deep into his lungs. He got up from his knees and tried to walk into that wall of fire, and it stopped him where reason could not . . .)

"I tore the boards away from the door and got it open, and then she came out. But it was too late . . ."

(Something black and shapeless flew out through the open doorway, hurtling past him. It was Samantha, and her long hair was a living torch. He threw himself on top of her, trying to smother the flames with his own body . . .)

"She was dying then, but she kept herself alive long enough to name one of them, the leader of the bunch. That's how I knew who they were." Blaine stared directly at Jessica Allen, his hard square face a mask in the darkness. "That's how I knew who to hunt."

Jessica Allen had listened with mounting horror, shocked by the depth of her own reaction to the grim tale. At the same time she tried numbly to comprehend Blaine's apparent coldness, the curt, unemotional way he had recounted the story. Did he really feel so little? Where was the grief? Had it burned away too?

But if that were true, why then did he still hunt the men who had killed his wife? Why track them down, intent on killing them? And for how long? Years, she guessed. Was it only anger that drove him? Or male pride? Or did she simply not understand how he had learned to cope with a pain and grief so terrible?

She shook her head despairingly. He was a strange, bitter man, all hard edges, no softness anywhere. How could she, a stranger to his life, expect to understand him?

And just as disturbing, why did her failure leave her feeling so unsettled? Why did it make her anxious?

"How long ago?" she whispered after a silence.

He did not answer, and she knew that she had pushed him as far as he would go.

There was a longer silence. The blackness of the canyon was absolutely still. Not a leaf stirred, nor did a bird call out. Suspended high above the canyon floor, with the darkness all around her, Jessica Allen had an eerie feeling of floating in space, cut off from the real world. The terror of Samantha Blaine so long ago lingered more vividly in her mind than the precarious reality of her own situation.

Then a tick of sound made Cullom Blaine grow rigid. She heard it too—a pebble dribbling down the face of the canyon. It came from far above them, and in the stillness the sound was like the roar of an avalanche. She tracked it all the way past the shelf where she lay until it vanished into the silence of the canyon bottom.

Almost immediately there was another faint scratching, like mice scurrying across an attic. Bits of dirt continued to filter down the steep wall of the canyon.

Jessica started to speak and Blaine clamped a hand over her mouth. He made an urgent hissing sound between his teeth. Then he moved his lips close to her ear, so close she could feel his warm breath. "Don't think about Apaches," he whispered. "Don't think about anything at all, about wanting to get away, about being scared or cold or hungry." As if he sensed her bewilderment he went on quickly. "Don't think on any of those things, because if you do he'll hear you. He'll know it, and he'll find us. Think of darkness or a meadow with flowers, or of nothing at all. Do you understand?"

There was another trickle of sound from above them. Not as far away this time. Jessica felt as if the trickling were along her spine.

Blaine shifted his body, pressing her down with his weight. She could feel the whole hard length of him against her. She felt his hand fumbling, searching, then finding something at his waist. He drew it out and she saw the gleam of a knife. Its blade caught what little light there was in this dark hollow.

He lay motionless, pressed against her, breathing in a low, shallow way so that she could not hear the sound of it even as close as she was. After a moment she was able to adjust her own breathing to his. Terrified, she lay rigid, knowing that someone—an Apache—was drawing closer to them, climbing cautiously down the slope in the darkness, searching . . .

15

The Apache had not moved for some minutes, long enough for Blaine to wonder if the disturbances he had heard high up the canyon wall had been made by some other kind of animal. Wishful thinking, he thought, rejecting the notion of an easy way out. When had he started grasping at straws of hope?

A whisper of movement removed the last doubt, if any truly remained. Had to be a young brave, Blaine thought, to let a moccasin slide against rock so noisily, or to kick pebbles out of his way. Young and eager and not destined to live to be old and reluctant.

He wasn't far above the shelf now, a little bit off to the left. No way of telling if the animal path or track he had searched out would bring him directly down upon Blaine's hiding place. No matter. It would bring him close enough to know that he wasn't alone. He wasn't young and foolish enough to be unable to smell a white man and woman only a few yards away.

Blaine's senses took over against his will, making him aware of every curve and dip of the woman's body pressed against his. She hadn't moved for quite a spell either, but he could feel the tension in her even as the heat of her thigh melted through their clothing and the pressure of her bosom against his chest stirred into life sensations long dormant, feelings that he didn't want to feel or even to recognize. He could smell that pleasant soapy scent from her body and the perfume of her hair . . .

He tried to concentrate on other things, like the feel of the canyon around him, the night sounds. You could sense life in the canyon at this quiet hour, motion in the stillness, soft rustlings, stirrings, natural sounds. They became part of the murmur of life, constant and mostly unnoticed, audible only in change. When something startled the small, quivery things into motionless silence.

But the thoughts he tried to shut off wouldn't stay quiet. Thoughts of hundreds of nights spent in remote places, almost always alone, watching solitary fires. He had become used to it, hardened, he supposed, so that he had come to expect nothing else. To ask for nothing else. It was the way of things.

There was even much about his way that he liked—had always liked but with the passing years had come to accept even more. There were moments and places you would not trade for any other. Moments in the early morning, the first sip of strong black coffee while the air was chill and unbelievably fresh. The sense of adventure that was always new in sighting upon a distant peak that he must reach. The peace that came sometimes when crossing a pretty mountain meadow where the grass was fresh and flowers spilled carelessly, and no trail marked the way, where both love and death seemed like ancient mysteries, as old as the surrounding mountains. The satisfaction of measuring himself, not against other men, but against the thunder and lightning, the tumbling rapids, the implacable forces of the land itself.

And he bowed to no man or woman. He went his own way, doing what he had to do.

But still alone.

And the woman pressed against him had awakened too

many memories, memories of soft whisperings on other distant nights, of quiet talks, of companionable silences. Memories of homely things, like the smell of fresh bread in the oven, the smell of dough on Samantha's hands . . .

With an effort Blaine once more forced his thoughts away from the woman. There was the young Shaker to think of. Would he get through? Blaine had been surprised that he was able to persuade Noah Calder to ride for help. He had a hunch that the young man's willingness had something to do with feeling useless in the fighting that had taken place at Cheever's Station. If he couldn't fire a gun in anger, at least he could try to get through to Fort Tracy where there were soldiers whose business it was to bear arms. He could do his part, carry his share of the load.

Though he had never subscribed to it, Blaine respected the nonviolent creed of the young Shaker couple, a belief familiar to him among Quakers he had known in his youth. He knew that it demanded a kind of strength of its own, the fortitude that let one go against the current regardless of what others might think or say. There were people—whole communities—who hated the Shakers for their strange customs and antics. Despised them for being different. Feared them because they didn't understand them. Holding true to what you believed in the face of such suspicion and even persecution asked for an uncommon integrity along with a rare kind of courage.

But when all that was said, Cullom Blaine still could not see the sense of it. He was a peaceful man himself—or had been once. And perhaps in the settled, civilized places of the East, where manners were held in higher esteem than physical courage or strength or skill with a gun, it was possible to hold your own place in the world without having to fight for it. Perhaps.

But not in the West, Blaine thought. The meek might one day inherit this land, but they would not tame and settle it. Here turning the other cheek was just not practical. You fought for what you had if someone tried to take it away from you. If you didn't, you wouldn't hold on to it very long. You hanged the horse thief without wringing your hands over it. You went after the men who murdered your wife and child . . .

And yet Blaine had heard of Quakers being friends among the Indians as they strove to be among all men, going into the camps and villages and living peacefully with the savages. They had first won the trust and confidence of Eastern tribes, and their reputation had gone before them as they came west. Would renegade Apaches honor that unwritten rule of acceptance where the young Shaker was concerned? He looked and acted enough like a Quaker to be one and the same as far as an Indian was concerned. Would Apaches recognize him for what he was? Would Navaja and his renegades?

Blaine could not even guess at the answer. It was something Noah Calder would have to find out for himself.

The Apache moved once more. This time Blaine did not hear the small disturbance of dust drifting down toward him; he smelled it. The Indian was creeping more cautiously now, inching down the face of the canyon.

To Blaine that meant only one thing. The Apache had sensed that someone was there, close by.

Noah Calder rode south, at first picking his way through broken hills in the darkness, then gradually quickening his pace as the land opened out and the dark thinned and he could make out the separate shapes of rocks and trees, the white thread of the trail he followed, the gray band that separated land from sky.

The buckskin needed little guidance over rough terrain. He was a big horse, sure-footed, with a comfortable gait. Noah liked the feel of the powerful animal between his legs, the long ground-eating stride when they hit an open stretch and Noah gave him rein, the responsiveness to the slightest pressure of his rider's hands or legs. Noah had never ridden a horse as swift and strong and intelligent. Any man would take pride in owning such a horse.

The thought reminded him of Cullom Blaine's actions toward the Apaches who had circled Noah and Charity in their little wagon. Blaine could have shot one or more of the Indians. He could easily have killed their leader's spirited horse. Instead he had fired only warning shots at the feet of their horses. At the time Noah had not completely understood the way the confrontation played out, but he guessed that Cullom Blaine had tried to give the Apaches a way out of the situation with minimal loss of pride. Blaine had said something briefly about the chief placing more value on his horse than on a pair of scalps.

Blaine undoubtedly felt the same about his buckskin. Yet he had turned the horse over to Noah without hesitation. The knowledge filled Noah with an uneasy pride. Uneasy because he felt less confidence in himself as he rode than Blaine had obviously placed in him.

Ever since crossing the Mississippi Noah had had a growing sense of being a misfit, as out of place as a sinner at a prayer meeting. His clothes set him apart. His youth and lack of experience had never been so obvious. His ignorance of the West, of cows and cowboys, of Indians and guns, stamped him a greenhorn on sight.

He was aware of the vastness of the land all around him, the raw bleak face of it compared to the forested places of his youth, so green and pleasant and cool. He felt puny and insignificant in this harsh and empty Plains country, and he could not help thinking with a tug of longing of the safe, sheltered community he and Charity had left behind. There had always been such a sense of serenity, orderliness, closeness in the community. The discipline of the Shaker society created its own feeling of security. One's place was always known. Even one's thoughts were guided.

Yet he had felt stifled there, Noah reminded himself. Especially after he fell in love with Charity. The rigid conformity of the community had inhibited natural desires, stifled ideas, smothered individual aspirations. There had been warmth and love, but these too had been corseted.

How different this all was! It was frightening, sometimes dangerous. There was no orderliness here, no sense of security. This was a savage wilderness, not a disciplined society. But what a sense of freedom filled him! He gazed around in wonder as he rode in the predawn dark, the wind cool against his face, the gaunt hills with their deep shadows filled with mystery. Life here would be at hazard every day; just surviving would be a constant battle. And in acknowledging this, confronting it, Noah felt a desire to live, to share all the terrors of their future here with Charity, a desire more intense than anything he had known. It was as if the very challenges and dangers made the possibilities of life sweeter.

Riding down a long slope, Noah saw the land opening out before him onto a level plain, a table whose far edge was just faintly visible. At this moment it was a land of blacks and grays, the hooded black of the hills melting into the gray of lowering clouds. At ground level it remained too dark to see much; Noah could make out patches of scrub brush and little else. He welcomed the coming of the day, the first graying along the eastern horizon at the far rim of the plain, for in the first stages of his ride his heart had jumped every time a shadow moved. But the coming of light would bring new risks. The darkness had sheltered him, hidden him from the eyes of the Indians.

What would he do if daylight brought him face to face with one or more of the warlike Apaches? It was a question that had been at the back of his mind since he had left Cheever's Station behind. He was determined to get through to Fort Tracy, or to find the soldiers on the way. *He had to!* But he knew that that might mean taking a stand somewhere along the line. How far could he go in defending himself? Here in the wilderness the neat questions of right and wrong, of refusing to kill or inflict harm on another human being no matter what the provocation, did not offer the neat answers he had been accustomed to accepting. Perhaps because death was simply more commonplace here, violence more an ordinary part of the pattern of life and of nature.

An Apache wouldn't let him decide for himself whether he would fight or not, Noah thought. If he was going to survive—if he was going to be able to bring the help needed for Charity and the others at Cheever's Station—he was going to have to deal with that.

And Noah meant to survive.

Reaching the bottom of the long slope, Noah turned the buckskin's head south once more. He had ridden only a few minutes when his heartbeat quickened. He came upon the trail left behind by more than a score of horses, also heading south. The cavalry!

Almost instantly his excitement was chilled. He peered more closely at the hoof marks in the white dust of the plain. Cavalry? he wondered. Or Apaches?

Noah realized that a man like Blaine would know. He

would be able to look down at the sign on the ground and read it, identifying hostiles or friendly soldiers.

"Thee has much to learn," Noah muttered to himself. "If thee would stay alive in this wilderness, thee had better start learning."

And he got down off the buckskin, crouching in the dim light to study the tracks on the ground.

Well to the north, on a clifftop high above Cheever's Station, Navaja knelt beside the small pyramid of wood he had gathered, a mix of dry and green twigs. The green would add smoke to his fire. He used two pieces of flint from his warbag to strike sparks into the nest at the heart of his stack. After several minutes a spark caught and he blew upon it, fanning it into a steady glow.

Smoke began to rise in a thin column. Though it was still too dark for the smoke to be seen clearly above the line of the hills over any distance, the message of the smoke must be seen at first light. And already the sky was graying to the east, the home of the Comanches.

Navaja waited patiently.

16

Tom and Art Clancy never saw the rider clearly, but they saw his dust in time. When Art first made out the dust it was still far enough off for them to veer away from their own trail and melt into the hills to the west.

Afraid of betraying their presence in the same way the other rider had, Art led the way across a gravel wash and pulled up behind a huge piece of driftwood that blocked the mouth of a canyon, letting rocks and debris pile up behind it. Art dismounted and looped his horse's reins over one of the bleached branches sticking up from the fallen trunk.

"Stay here and watch the horses," he told Tom, who always felt better when he had spelled out for him what to do.

Art trotted forward to a great mound of seamed and fissured rock and quickly clambered up to the top. Lying flat, he peered out at the wide plain stretching below him to the east. The drift of dust he had spotted was there, all right. Just one rider, Art concluded after a moment. In the poor light he hadn't been sure at first. But there wasn't enough dust for more than one horse.

The cavalry lieutenant hadn't sent out any scouts that morning. And it didn't seem likely that many other white men would be out this way alone, considering all the recent rumors of Indian troubles.

It added up to an Apache. Possibly a scout trailing the

cavalry. Maybe just a hunter. Whatever, the dust he left behind showed he was heading south.

Art relaxed. He took the time to fish paper and tobacco from his shirt pocket. Using only his left hand he rolled a cigarette, twisting the end neatly to avoid spilling any tobacco. He cupped his hand to shield the flame from his match. It was Art's first cigarette of the day, and he drew the smoke into his lungs with conscious pleasure.

Maintaining his vantage point on top of the rock while he smoked, Art turned his head to see Tom watching him. Tom had been more jittery than usual this morning. He hadn't wanted to leave the cavalry camp before daylight, and he'd spent much of their first hour's ride muttering protests.

The truth was that Art had chosen to spend the night in the camp of the cavalry patrol as much to calm his brother down as for any other reason. Tom hated Indians, Apaches even more than Comanches, and the hate was inspired by fear. He had been as jumpy as water in a hot pan ever since they had crossed the Pecos, the two of them riding west alone. Tom had been all for waiting east of the river until the bounty hunter, Rimmer, joined them. Art had had to point out patiently more than once that Cullom Blaine was heading west, not east. Unless they kept dogging his heels he would be long gone. But if they joined up with Rimmer as soon as possible and kept after Blaine, they had a chance of catching Blaine before he could elude pursuit. At least they'd be close enough to see which way he jumped.

Funny thing was that Tom wasn't nearly as scared of Cullom Blaine as he was of Apaches. And Blaine, Art thought, might prove more dangerous.

Art saw the dark shape of the unknown rider as he galloped past the mouth of the canyon where the brothers had concealed themselves. He was a fleeting shadow, gone in an instant, and in that brief, unsatisfactory glimpse Art could not say for certain whether the rider had been an Indian or not.

When the dust trail the rider left behind—would an Apache ride so openly?—had drifted well past the canyon, Art slid down from the huge rock and returned to his horse. "He's gone," Art said. "Let's ride."

"Who was it?" Tom asked anxiously. "Apaches?"

"Don't know," Art answered brusquely. "But it was only one man, and he's movin' fast, headin' south. Could be he's tracking the cavalry."

"I tol' you we shouldn't of left till it was daylight," Tom complained. "You never listen to me."

"I will when you say somethin' useful," Art snapped.

"Well, we coulda waited for breakfast anyways." Tom was convinced that the cavalry ate like kings compared to the spartan fare the brothers carried with them, mostly beans and salt pork.

"You can eat a cow when we get to Cheever's Station," Art said. "It can't be much farther now."

He climbed into the saddle and turned his gelding around the driftwood pile. Tom followed along behind as Art led them back to the trail they had been following earlier. There was no longer any sign of the lone rider who had passed them by. He had vanished into the lingering darkness of the plain. Art thought he could still smell dust in the air but that might have been his imagination.

In the few minutes they had holed up at the mouth of the canyon the shadows had begun to lift a little from the land. It wouldn't be long before the first streaks of flame lanced the eastern horizon, as if dawn were a bloodletting. Then maybe Tom would stop his grumbling, Art thought.

They had been riding only a short time when, squinting ahead along the trail that led northwest toward Cheever's Station, Art saw something that brought a tightening to his own chest. He knew Tom hadn't seen it yet, and it gave Art a perverse satisfaction to call it to his brother's attention.

"Look ahead there, Tom. You see what I see?"

"What the hell—?" With a sharp gasp Tom involuntarily pulled up.

A thin, broken column of smoke rose against the gray morning sky. Not far off, Art thought. It climbed above the hills about where he expected to reach Cheever's Station.

Lieutenant Arnold Wilson had been aroused early by the small sounds the pair of drifters had made while pulling out of the camp long before first light. He heard one of the men curse as he blundered over some obstacle in the darkness. Then there were the unmistakable leathery creakings and tuggings of horses being saddled.

Wilson shrugged his blankets aside. Instantly he felt the sharp early morning chill. As he stood he saw that Private Enos Slaton, the sentry on duty at the south end of the camp by the picket line, was alert, watching the two strangers as they mounted and made ready to leave the camp.

Lieutenant Wilson relaxed. With the easing of his mood he realized that something about the two strangers had made him uneasy enough to cause his sleep to be light, broken and restless much of the night. He slapped his arms around his body, beating off the chill and the sluggishness left over from his ragged sleep.

The two strangers—Clancy was the name both used, he reminded himself, not certain why the reminder was necessary—saw him watching them as they clopped around the camp with its still-sleeping forms and swung north. Neither man spoke out. Wilson raised his hand but there was no acknowledgment. He watched them leave in silence.

He wondered why they were so eager to be up early and on the trail—in the manner of men on the dodge, he thought. Yet wanted men would hardly have ridden so boldly into an army camp and asked to stay the night.

They seemed shifty-eyed, untrustworthy types, but that was all he really had against them. Wilson had nothing to go on but his instinct, but he knew for a certainty that they were not the kind of men to turn your back on. Or trust out of sight. Neither man had said or done anything untoward while at the patrol's camp, but . . .

The early hour remained dark even after the sounds of hoofbeats had faded off. What was it they had asked him about? Cheever's Station. They had been interested in who was there, and whether the stage had arrived. They were also worried about Indian troubles. Arnold Wilson had had little information to give them, and even less inclination to provide it. Still, maybe he was being unfair.

His restlessness persisted long after the Clancy brothers had ridden off. Wilson sat by the coals of the campfire and drank thick black coffee—"Strong enough to polish boots," Owen Claymore, his sergeant with the patrol, had joked. At least it would help wake him up, maybe get rid of this sleep-clogged feeling.

By the time Arnold Wilson had finished his coffee and tossed the dregs at the fire, he had come to admit to himself that something other than the Clancy brothers was bothering him. He caught sight of Beaver Sampson, trudging back into the camp after relieving himself, and called him over. "You having breakfast, Sampson?"

The scout shrugged indifferently. "Don't eat much in the mornin'," he said. "It's like me an' my belly don't agree on what's a good time. It says mornin' is a bad time."

"When you're ready," the lieutenant said slowly, "I'd like you to back-trail us a ways. Scout into those hills and see if you come across anything out of the way . . . any sign of . . . whatever."

"Navaja?"

Wilson shrugged. "His name has come up more than once. I'm certain we would have had some earlier word if he was out making trouble, but . . ."

"You got a feelin', Lieutenant?"

Arnold Wilson looked at the wiry little scout with quick suspicion, searching for any glint of amusement in the bright blue eyes or lurking behind the salt-and-pepper beard. He saw only a keen, waiting interest. "I reckon you could say that," he admitted. "It's like something is bothering me, something I should have taken more notice of . . ."

Beaver Sampson regarded him with some approval. Contrary to the lieutenant's wary concern, Sampson had a healthy respect for intuition, the gut feeling that told a man when something was not what it was supposed to be, or warned him of danger when there was nothing in sight to cause alarm. It was not something the scout would snicker at. Many times such a feeling was more valuable and reliable than physical evidence, especially when soldiering, when you were often dealing with sudden and unexpected dangers in hostile territory. Beaver Sampson credited such "belly knowledge," as he called it, with having saved his life more than once. That this West Pointer would even admit to listening to such whispers increased his grudging respect for the young officer. Maybe he'd do, after all.

"Those two hardcases botherin' you, Lieutenant?"

"No, not really—but you might make sure they are traveling where they said. I don't trust them much."

Beaver Sampson nodded, feeling that the judgment hardly required comment.

"You'll still be headin' on in to the fort?"

"I see no reason not to. We're low on rations and due to report to Command in any event," Arnold Wilson replied. "I see no reason to delay. At least . . . not yet."

"I'll be headin' out soon as I lubricate my tonsils," the scout said. He seldom ate much in the morning, but he would sooner do without whiskey than miss his first mug of coffee every day.

"The horses will be pulling as soon as they sense we're heading back," Wilson said. "But we won't be moving out until full light. You shouldn't have any problem catching up. And if you come across anything, anything at all, report to me as soon as you can."

"I'll let you know, Lieutenant," Sampson said. "Ain't likely I'll be in any hurry, but if I am I can give the telegraph a head start and still get there first."

The officer smiled for the first time that morning.

17

With the approach of daylight, Clay Adams watched the man called Rimmer with mingled feelings of fear and resentment. It was the fear he resented. Even Indians had never made him shake in his boots.

Rimmer had made him back down. Rimmer had let him see his own death. He wondered if he would ever again completely shake the vision.

He watched as Rimmer, scowling, paced the floor, moving sometimes to the front window to peer out, impatiently waiting for dawn to steal away the shadows. He would kill Blaine, Adams knew, as soon as it was light.

Rimmer's gaze caught his, surprised the naked resentment. Rimmer's upper lip curled. He stared at Adams until the stage driver dropped his eyes.

The young Shaker girl had seen the exchange, Adams thought, a flush mounting hot on his neck. He was glad the comely widow from Fort Tracy wasn't there to watch his humiliation.

Shamefaced, he quickly reminded himself that the thought was unworthy. She was somewhere in the surrounding hills, taken by Blaine against her will. He wished her no harm.

Maybe Blaine would kill Rimmer.

The brief hope awakened by the thought flickered out as quickly as it came. As far as anyone knew, Blaine was unarmed. But even if Blaine had a gun, Clay Adams doubted that he could survive a shoot-out with Rimmer. Blaine was a badman, sure—he hadn't hesitated to gun down the marshal when he had the chance, shooting him in the back—but Rimmer had put him belly-up there in the barn when Blaine had a gun in his hand. Cut him down and kicked him in the head like he was nothing.

Those holsters tied low to Rimmer's legs told their own story. But it was the gunman's eyes that had chilled Adams to the bone, turning his knees to water and his will to jelly.

Adams shivered.

It seemed like a long time—only two days—since he and Ben Crisler had pulled up at Cheever's Station. In that brief span he had flirted with two women, helped to fight off a band of Apaches, and learned that he was a coward. What other name could he put on it?

His stagecoach partner had fared even worse. Poor Ben had been tortured while he was still alive, hacked to pieces. Clay had been sick to his stomach after helping to carry Ben's body. It lay wrapped in sheeting now in a corner of the barn, awaiting decent burial.

Maybe it would be safe enough to bury him in the morning. Rimmer seemed convinced the Apaches had no stomach for more fighting, and Clay Adams wasn't about to argue with him.

He'd be glad to get out of this place, away from Rimmer. Far enough away so he could try to forget that queasiness he had felt in his belly when Rimmer challenged him.

Some people are able to slide through life, surrounded by all manner of hazards, by danger, death and diseases, without being touched by it, or without being deeply affected. Clay Adams had always been one of those.

It wasn't that he hadn't known some hardship, growing

up in a family of hardscrabble Georgia farmers. But he and his brothers had never gone hungry. His two older brothers had even survived the war without loss of limb or serious injury, and Clay himself had been a boy, too young to be in the fighting or even to understand the bitter futility of it.

After the war and growing toward manhood, Clay had drifted west, a happy-go-lucky youth whose good looks and good nature made him welcome wherever he went. He had been in some scrapes, fought bare-knuckled now and then and held his ground, and even been a participant in several fights with Kiowas and Comanches. He had always come through unscathed.

Women liked him. He fancied—not without reason—that their eyes followed him when he sauntered by. He had bought his twill pants and gingham shirt from a dry goods merchant in Fort Worth. His fine boots were custom-made, and his Stetson had set him back nearly a whole summer's wages. He cut an attractive figure with his clothes and his tall, lean-hipped, wide-shouldered body and his engaging grin.

It was his image of himself that had suffered irretrievable damage in the confrontation with Rimmer.

Rimmer stopped pacing abruptly. Clay Adams shot a quick glance at him. Adams was sitting, and one of his legs began to jerk up and down a little. He put his hand on it and tried to stop the nervous bouncing, silently cursing his jumpiness.

"Cheever?" Rimmer called out. "Where's that damn Woman? Where's the coffee?"

"It's comin' up," Cheever answered in a surly tone.

For the first time Clay Adams smelled the aroma of coffee from the kitchen and it set the juices flowing in his mouth. He wanted coffee and he was also hungry. He'd had no stomach for food the night before.

No stomach for anything, he told himself bitterly.

"Be light soon," Rimmer muttered, once again at the front window to peer out at the shadows. The night still looked black to Adams, but he knew Rimmer was right. There was an eagerness in Rimmer that became more visible as dawn drew closer. *He likes killing. He can't wait for it.*

Woman emerged from the kitchen with coffee in a huge pot and some hard rolls. The station began to stir, Rimmer turning away from the window toward the Indian, Chandler sitting up and rubbing his eyes, Cheever lighting another of the coal-oil lamps. Adams was glad of the activity.

He waited until Rimmer had turned back to the window before he went to get a cup of coffee for himself.

Charity Calder waited anxiously for the long night to end. It was the first night she and Noah had been apart since leaving the Ohio community.

She thought of the nights back there in the communal house, lying in a roomful of women, most of them older than she, all of them, she was certain, with hearts and minds taken up only with the goodness of God and the joy of life in His service. While she lay thinking only of Noah, who slept with the men in the far side of the house. Forbidden thoughts.

Wanting to be with him.

Now she shuddered, appalled by her own courage in letting him ride off alone into a night peopled by savages, men who found pride and joy in hacking another to pieces. That wasn't exactly how Mr. Blaine had described them, but that was what it came down to.

If Noah did not get through safely, if he did not return to her, she would have no desire to live. She had given up a whole way of life to be with him, and learned that she had made a good bargain. Depriving her of his love would be like denying a plant water. She would shrivel and die.

But if Blaine was right about the Apaches, she might not survive anyway. She had faced that knowledge when Noah came to her, indecisive, wanting to go but not wanting to leave her. All she would have had to do was gently tell him she was afraid to be left alone. He would not have gone.

It was a terrible power to have, she thought.

She had watched the evil Rimmer exercising a different kind of power over others, the power of fear, and been both shocked and angered. Oddly, he did not frighten her.

Only the possibility of Noah not returning could strike terror into her heart.

She shook her head when the Indian Woman offered coffee, shook it more firmly when Cheever tried to press a cup upon her. She was needed in the sleeping room, where the wounded man, Sanderson, had been moved. His bandages would have to be changed again.

She rose, a slender figure in her long dress, and moved with a quiet dignity toward the sleeping room. All of the men in the station paused in what they were doing, watching in silence until she disappeared through the door.

A hundred feet into the canyon, and halfway up its east wall, Cullom Blaine and Jessica Allen waited. The skyline was visible now, a grayness above the ridgetops, but the first light of day had not yet penetrated the blackness of the canyon. It wouldn't be long now, he thought, and when it came the light would wash through the canyon with the swiftness of a flash flood.

The Apache had been still for a long, long time. Waiting them out. He knows, Blaine thought. He doesn't know where we are but he knows someone is here. He's just waiting for daylight.

Blaine could make out the woman's features now, separate the honey of her hair from the similar coloring of the rock wall behind their shelf. There were dark smudges under her eyes. Small lines there too. Had she laughed often with her soldier husband? Or squinted against the sun, shielding her eyes as she watched the horizon for his return?

And why in hell was he thinking such thoughts at such a time? Or any time?

Jessica Allen saw his scowl, the way he turned away to peer up-canyon. Too dark to see anything yet. Why had he frowned, his eyes upon her? Was he wishing her elsewhere?

It had been so long since there was any sound at all that she could almost believe no Indian was there above them in the darkness. But she knew enough about such canyons to realize that the total absence of any breath of life was itself unnatural. Even the birds were silent this morning.

And she trusted Cullom Blaine's judgment. Trusted it instinctively, without analyzing that trust. It was a thing he would know, she thought. Simply that.

During the hours of waiting her attitude toward Blaine had undergone a dramatic change. It was as if she had come to know him far better than their brief acquaintance justified. They were so tightly pressed together in the narrow space that she felt she knew every contour of his solid, muscular frame. She believed that she was beginning to know how he thought, how his mind worked.

Her sense of the quiet strength of him had grown even as she became more uncomfortably conscious of the heat of his body. She felt simultaneously pushed and pulled. Anger struggled to hold its claim—he had struck her. What was so different about his and Joe Allen's blows? (Blaine had done it only because he had to, a voice whispered, and then reluctantly.) But other emotions diluted the anger, thinned it out, finally washed it away.

How much had Blaine left unsaid about his wife's death? She realized now that he had not spoken callously, without feeling anything; he was simply the kind of man who hid such feelings from view.

And could she blame him for going after his poor wife's murderers, hunting them down one by one? Wouldn't she want *her* man to do as much for her? He was in no way to be judged the same as the sly gunman who had killed Joe Allen. Over a game of cards.

Blaine stirred, shifting position. She could feel the texture of his worn jeans brushing against her leg, and the sensation made her flinch. She was dismayed by her body's reactions, its selfish awareness of Blaine as a man. Her response seemed . . . disloyal. Dishonest. Improper.

Almost at once she knew that it was none of these things. Joe was dead, her love for him had died a long time before. She had stayed with him out of loyalty. The feelings she had now, whatever they were, were not disloyal. Or dishonest.

Damn it, she *liked* Cullom Blaine!

He stirred her as no man had since she was a young woman bewitched by Joe Allen's reckless grin. It made little sense. Here she was lying on a stone ledge, badly frightened, possibly as close to death as she had ever come, and what was she worrying about? The savage who lurked in the darkness of the canyon, waiting to kill her as well as Blaine? No, she worried about her feelings toward a brooding man to whom she meant nothing at all, to whom she was merely an inconvenience.

Or was that fair? He could have been shed of her at any time earlier. He could have abandoned her once he had escaped. He had kept her with him because he wouldn't leave her to the merciless cruelty of the Apaches.

Beyond that, she reminded herself, he could have taken his horse instead of giving it to Noah Calder with instructions to ride for help. Why hadn't he? Because he wouldn't abandon the people at Cheever's Station while he still believed it to be under attack? Because he wouldn't run out on them, people who had been so quick to turn against him, believing the worst? My God, how could she judge such a man for anything he had done in the past? How could she blame him?

She felt a sharp pressure from Blaine's elbow. Turning to glare at him, she saw that he was watching her. The elbow had been to get her attention.

He brought his mouth close to her ear. She felt his warm breath and shivered in spite of herself. "He's waiting us out," Blaine whispered, so low she could hardly hear him. "He knows we're here."

Jessica nodded, not trusting herself to speak.

"I'll have to go after him. Can't wait here for him to find us."

"You . . . you have no gun . . ."

"I have a knife. And you can help even things up."

Jessica swallowed. Her mouth was dry. "How?" she whispered.

"Give me ten minutes, no more. It won't matter if you're a little early or late. Then I want you to climb down."

She shook her head quickly. "I . . . I don't think I can."

"You can. And don't try to do it quietly. Make as much noise as you can. Make it sound as if you're in a desperate hurry."

"I will be." She managed a smile.

Blaine studied her. Was there an answering smile in his eyes? She couldn't be sure.

"Ten minutes. When you get to the bottom, run for the station. Don't look back—just run!"

Jessica Allen nodded. Her heart had already started drumming in her chest.

She turned on her side in order to watch him as he eased off the shelf. But a moment later he had climbed out of sight, disappearing around the brow of rock that covered her shelter.

She waited, forcing herself to count slowly, not trusting her sense of time, which seemed to have vanished completely. One minute. Two. Was that whisper a foot sliding over rock? Or only her imagination? How could a man so big move so quietly that she had not heard a sound once he slipped out of her sight?

She saw his boots, standing mutely next to the wall near her feet. She hadn't realized he had taken them off before he slipped away. She shivered. The empty boots made the danger more real, brought it closer.

How long now? Five minutes? Oh dear God, she had lost count, let herself be distracted. But surely she had not lost more than a minute, and Blaine had made it clear that a minute or two would not matter.

She resumed her count, trying to concentrate, to ignore the heavy, almost painful slam of her heart against her ribs, the constriction in her throat, the pounding in her temples. How could she hear anything over that tumult?

Eight minutes. She began to get ready.

She did not wait the full ten minutes. As soon as the number nine tolled in her brain she rolled over the edge of the shelf and started down, feet first, facing the steep wall. She slid and caught at a bush, scrambled down a few more feet, felt a pointed rock scrape along her body. From above her came a bloodcurdling yell. It made the hairs rise on the back of her neck. In panic she tried to climb down more quickly. She lost her grip, skidded out of control. Then she seemed to drop over a sharp edge into a void. She tumbled toward the floor of the canyon in a noisy slide of dirt and rock.

18

After stumbling upon the tracks of a large band of horses, Noah Calder followed them for nearly a quarter of an hour before the fact registered in his mind that the hoof-marks were similar to those made by the buckskin he rode. They had been made by shod horses.

Although Noah was not completely certain of his memory, he had an idea that the tracks of the horses ridden by the Indians he had encountered on the way to Cheever's Station were unlike these. Apaches probably rode unshod ponies. At least he had never heard of an Indian black-smith.

Noah was confident that the cavalry had ridden this way. Theirs were the tracks he followed. Moreover, it had rained yesterday around midafternoon. These tracks had been made since then; they cut deeper into the wet earth.

Unless the troopers had kept in the saddle all night, Noah told himself, they couldn't be that far ahead of him. They were traveling south, same as he was, presumably heading toward Fort Tracy. With any kind of luck at all he should be able to catch up to them.

"This is where we make a run," Noah murmured aloud to the big buckskin.

With each passing moment the day grew lighter on the open plain. The sun's glow was visible just above the hori-zon, a band of brightness trapped between a ripple of low hills in the far distance and the gray cloud layer. It was a special moment of transient beauty before the rising sun disappeared once more behind the clouds.

In the blooming light Noah found it easier to follow the wide swath left by the cavalry less than twenty-four hours ago. He let the buckskin run freely. He leaned low over the horse's neck, gripping the reins with one hand and holding onto his hat with the other after it almost blew off. His long coat, left unbuttoned when he first mounted, flapped and fluttered behind him like a giant cape billowing on the wind. There was an exhilaration in the run, the pounding ride coupled with the heady possibility of danger and his growing excitement over the conviction that he would do it all—find the soldiers, save Cheever's Station, save Charity!

After about a half hour Noah slowed the buckskin's reckless and punishing gallop, realizing that even this big strong horse could not go on running all out without letup. Noah's gaze searched the empty prairie. Was that dust he could see to the south, a smudge of white hugging the ground? Or were his eyes deceiving him, his hopes racing ahead of reality?

Moments later the tracks veered to the right and milled in a circle. Noah pulled up. A brief search revealed the black ashes of a single fire. There was water nearby at the foot of the hills from a spring-fed stream. Noah didn't think the patrol had camped here overnight. More likely they had stopped for a rest before moving on. With his newfound eye for such things Noah calculated that there were not enough horse droppings for an overnight stop. There would have been a bigger campfire, perhaps several fires. They had stopped here in the afternoon—after it rained—before making camp somewhere up ahead later in the day.

Noah stopped by the stream long enough to let the

buckskin drink a little, but the big horse seemed to know without Noah's urging that it wasn't the time to have his fill.

Noah felt his empty stomach growling. He banished the thought resolutely. It wouldn't hurt him to go hungry. He wasn't far behind the patrol now.

Climbing back into the saddle, Noah swung away from the bivouac area. Something made him cast a glance upward toward the hills to the west. From the top of a long bench about a hundred feet above him, a lone figure on horseback gazed down at him.

Noah's heart seemed to stop. An Indian!

The Apache sat astride a short-legged, yellow-brown pony with a dark mane. The Indian wore only fringed buckskin leggings and moccasins. From the waist up he was naked except for a bright red strip of cloth tied in a band around his head and holding his long black hair in place.

Although they were on different planes, Noah on the lower level and the Apache high above him, the distance between them in direct line of sight was not great. Noah was able to see the coppery color of the savage's skin and daubs of red, black and ocher paint slashing across his cheeks and the bridge of his nose. He could see the thick pads of muscle beneath the skin of the man's chest and arms, even the tight line of his mouth—a forbidding expression that reminded Noah of some of the elders in the Shaker community.

But this Indian was young—no older than Noah himself, he thought in that instant of recognition—and he looked like what he was, a perfectly trained and conditioned warrior.

With an explosion of breath Noah Calder jabbed his

heels into the buckskin's flanks. The big horse took off in a
violent series of jumps—almost throwing his rider—before settling into a strong gallop. Flashing a glance over
his shoulder, Noah saw the Indian leap into action. He
raced along the top of the bench parallel to Noah's course.
The Apache's smaller pony, wiry and muscular as its rider,
ran with catlike speed, and the buckskin could not pull
ahead.

Moments later the Apache disappeared from view. The
buckskin ran on, showing no signs of fatigue. Noah
slapped his hat—still gripped in his hand after nearly flying off earlier—against his thigh as he had seen a cowboy
do, and whooped with triumph.

Peering ahead, squinting—his eyes watered with the
rush of wind against them as he raced on—it seemed to
Noah that the low cloud of white dust he had seen earlier,
far to the south, was more distinct. The dust had to be the
patrol! No way the Apache would catch up or intercept
him now. He—

Noah hardly heard the shot. There was only a small
sound like a slap. He jerked a glance toward the hills. The
bench had tilted downward. Noah saw to his dismay that
it turned into a long ramp that led down to the level plain
—the slope even made the Apache's run easier.

They were on a collision course. Near the bottom of the
natural ramp the Apache suddenly veered to his left, cutting down a steep trough etched into the slope. The wiry
Indian pony skidded, front legs stiff against a fall, easily
kept its feet and scrambled onto safe terrain.

The Apache was close now—a lot closer than Noah had
thought possible. He flew forward at an angle that cut
across Noah's path. And as he rode he whipped a rifle to
his shoulder!

Noah saw the puff of smoke from the muzzle of the rifle,

dimly heard the *whack!* of the shot. In panic he jerked the reins. The buckskin broke stride and plunged to his left.

The move let the Apache race in front of them. Noah was being forced to his left, out into the open. There was no refuge anywhere in sight. Close to the hills were clumps of brush and mesquite—beyond was only short grass. The buckskin might yet outrun the Indian's pony, but he could not outrun a bullet.

Feeling trapped, Noah pulled up. He was breathing hard, his heart slamming against his ribs. The buckskin danced a little, blowing, still excited, still eager to run, and Noah had all he could do to control him.

The Apache wheeled around him, the dark, painted face split by a wide grin, white teeth gleaming against the copper skin. Suddenly he charged forward. Noah tried to pull away but he was not quick enough. The young warrior was upon him in a flash, his body leaning forward and away from his pony. He cut across Noah's flank, reached out—and touched him as he flew by!

Noah stared in astonishment as the Apache circled him again. A superb rider, the Indian had his pony doing a kind of prance, while he broke into a strange, shrill yell that Noah could only understand as a cry of triumph.

Anger brought heat to Noah's face. He was unarmed, helpless, and the savage was taunting him! Knowing he had nothing to fear! Familiarity with the Apache had grown in the last few moments, convincing Noah that this was one of the three Indians who had circled him and Charity in their wagon the day Cullom Blaine had so fortuitously appeared. Maybe the young brave felt that Noah had got away once and he was going to make sure it didn't happen again.

Once more the Apache darted in at Noah. This time Noah dodged aside, urging the buckskin into an agile leap.

Anger and frustration and mounting fear made Noah's thoughts whirl. What could he do? Run for it across the open plain? Take a chance that the Indian would not shoot to kill? It seemed a forlorn, desperate hope.

Swiftly the Indian drove at Noah again, eager to score another coup. But as he leaned out to touch his enemy, the young Shaker surprised him. Instead of ducking away as he had before, when the Apache plunged past him Noah reached out, grabbed the barrel of the Indian's rifle, and hung on.

Surprise worked for him. The Apache had not been expecting any such move from an enemy so quick to flee. He had been holding his rifle in one hand, his pony's reins in the other, and his grip on the rifle was not as firm as it might have been. Noah jerked the weapon free. The barrel was still warm as his hand wrapped around it.

But Noah's hasty grip was not secure. As the Apache spun his pony around and came after him, Noah tried to elude the charge and at the same time pull the rifle out of reach. Instead it flew out of his hand. The rifle landed with the butt of the stock down. It did a crazy rolling hop and skidded across the dusty floor of the plain.

"Eeeeih!" The Apache's shout this time was not of triumph but of rage—a warrior's battle cry.

He charged his pony directly at Noah. His hand dipped to his side and came up with a crudely made but menacing tomahawk, a weapon more frightening to Noah than the rifle, fashioned of a sharp-edged stone tightly strapped by leather thongs to the head of a sturdy wooden handle.

In his anger over losing his rifle, the Apache attacked before he had his war club ready. He struck prematurely and—luckily for Noah—the blow only grazed the Shaker's upper arm.

Even in a glancing near-miss Noah felt the brutal

weight of the tomahawk strike. Fear seized the back of Noah's neck like a cold hand. He acted without thinking— no question of right or wrong, of committing violence against another or refraining. When the Apache spun around to face him, Noah dug in his heels. The buckskin jumped forward, and Noah threw himself off his horse into the Apache.

His momentum bowled both of them off the Indian pony's back. They tumbled together to the ground. Noah grabbed at the savage's right arm, fearing the tomahawk.

In the first moment of surprise he had the advantage. The Apache had been thrown off balance mentally as well as physically. Noah rolled on top of him, wrenching at the war club. The stone head banged against his ribs, making him wince in pain. But then he had a strong hold on it. Noah's hands and arms, trained to farming and hard labor, were surprisingly powerful. He pulled the weapon out of the Apache's hand and threw it far out of reach.

Then he was fighting for his life.

Noah fought not in anger but out of fear, not to kill or maim but simply to survive. And once the Indian brave had recovered from his initial surprise, Noah had his hands full—more than he could handle. He was strong, but so was the Apache. The Indian was all hard muscle and bone, so agile and quick that he might have been made of coiled springs. And Noah was handicapped by his long coat, which seemed to want to wrap itself around him as he struggled.

Noah tried to get an armlock on his adversary but the Indian twisted free. He threw Noah off him and jumped to his feet. The Shaker youth was up almost as fast. He dove headfirst into the Indian, legs driving, and knocked him to the ground.

Blood pounded in Noah's head. He smashed a fist into

the other's face, feeling something yield, feeling the smear of blood on his knuckles. The Apache kneed him cruelly, and Noah doubled over in pain. He groaned aloud, a kind of sob, but as the Indian closed on him Noah struck him again, a solid blow that staggered the savage. There was a strange exhilaration in striking the blows that was unlike any Noah had felt before. There was no guilt or shame, there wasn't time for that, there was only the desperate need to survive and a fierce excitement that was new to him.

The wild fear had left him, but not the knowledge that he fought for his life—perhaps for Charity's life as well, and for all those he had left behind at Cheever's Station.

Noah thought of shucking his cumbersome coat, but he was afraid of getting his arms tangled in the sleeves, of being momentarily helpless when the Apache attacked again.

Both men were more cautious now, circling each other warily, caked with dust and each other's blood, breathing hard. No longer did the Apache mock him with laughter. There was something else in the way he watched Noah, something that Noah saw: a wary respect, that of one warrior for another. The perception stunned Noah.

"This is crazy!" he burst out. "I don't wish to harm thee —I am not your enemy!"

The Apache stared at him.

"We don't have to do this, but I will not have thee kill me without a fight. Maybe that's wrong, but that's the way it is."

But there was no understanding in the black eyes that glared back at him, no friendliness, no answering gesture of peace. It was no use, Noah thought; there was no way to call off the fight. The chasm between them could not be bridged with words.

He rushed at the Apache, who eluded the charge and tripped Noah up. Noah grabbed the Indian's leg as he fell, pulling him down. A moccasined foot slammed into the side of his head, momentarily stunning him, breaking his grip.

He shook off the second's confusion. He rolled, tasting dust, and scrambled clear.

He was on his hands and knees, rising to meet the next attack, when he saw the Apache scoop up the tomahawk Noah had taken from him moments before.

White teeth flashed in the dark face once more, not in derision or laughter but in a kind of snarl.

The Apache darted forward, forcing Noah to jump back. Twice more the Indian jumped at him, feinting Noah into awkward moves. The third time Noah tried to stand his ground while warding off a strike. He stumbled off balance. His long coat became tangled in his legs. The Apache leaped upon him, driving Noah onto his back.

The brave straddled him. Noah looked up into the Indian's painted face, into black eyes that were totally alien to him, fierce and proud and hard as agates, eyes without pity.

Their gazes locked for a taut moment as Noah strained to hold on to the Apache's right arm, the one wielding the deadly war club.

The Indian wrenched his arm free. The tomahawk rose high above Noah's head.

Neither fighter had seen or heard the approach of another man on horseback. The first awareness Noah had was the sharp crack of a rifle.

The Apache jerked backward as if struck by a heavy blow. A hole appeared at the base of his neck and immediately disappeared as a flower of red bloomed over the hole.

There was a second shot. The tomahawk slipped from the Apache's grasp, and he fell away.

Noah stared up at a scrawny, bearded man in dirty buckskins, calmly sitting astride a gray horse, a smoking rifle cradled across the pommel of his saddle.

Staggering to his feet, Noah looked from the stranger to the Indian dead at his feet. Unexpected tears blurred his vision. "Why did thee do it?" he choked. "Why did thee shoot him?"

"Well, now, it seemed like a good idea at the time," the rider drawled. "Course I coulda let him bury that tommyhawk in your skull."

"You didn't have to kill him!"

"Mebbe it woulda been more polite to ask him what he was fixin' to do. I jest didn't think of it at the time," the little man said amiably. His bright blue eyes flicked over Noah's shoulder, searching the hills behind him. "I suppose I could ask you what you was doin' wrestlin' with an Apache."

"He . . . he attacked me."

"That's the way I seen it too." Apparently satisfied that there were no other Indians in sight, the rider examined Noah more critically, taking in the dust and blood, the long gray coat, the wide-brimmed black hat lying on the ground nearby. "You was at Cheever's Station. Seen you come in, with a fine-lookin' woman. Ain't that right?"

Noah nodded, realizing the man intended a compliment rather than giving offense. Hesitantly he peered down at the body of the Apache. His eyes filled. This was the first time he had ever struck another, the only time he had ever fought for his life. But it was not the fight he regretted now, Noah realized; it was the Apache's violent death.

But had the man intended anything different for Noah himself?

"That your horse?"

Noah followed the rider's gaze toward the buckskin, which had drifted only a short distance. Noah tried to pull himself together. "Yes. I was riding after the cavalry patrol. There's been an attack—" A glimmer of understanding came. "You saw me? Were you with the cavalry?"

"That's right, son. They call me Beaver Sampson, scout for the army." The rider had shed his casual manner. "Why was you ridin' after soldiers?" he asked sharply. "Who's been attacked?"

"Cheever's Station!" Noah blurted out. The story came in a rush—how, two nights ago, Apaches had stolen horses from Cheever's corral while it was still dark, and followed up the raid with an early morning attack and sporadic fighting later in the day. "They were gone by nightfall, and most of the people at the station believe they have left for good. But Mr. Blaine thinks otherwise. That's his horse I was riding. He sent me after the patrol. He says it's Navaja leading the Apaches, that he has some grievance, and that he will not leave before he's done what he came for."

"I wonder what that is," Beaver Sampson murmured. But the speculation occupied him only for an instant. "Reckon Blaine is right. Lucky I come on you when I did." For the first time his glance touched the dead Apache; his eyes showed no regret. "Unlucky for him—an' mebbe for Navaja. You able to ride, son?"

"Yea. I would thank thee for saving my life . . ." Noah broke off, his words stumbling once more over the harsh fact of the Apache's death and his role in it.

"No time for that," Sampson said curtly. "I'll be ridin' hell for leather, I can't wait for you. You follow as quick as you can. You'll be seein' the patrol's dust to the south. Head straight for it and we'll be comin' to meet you." He wheeled the gray but hesitated briefly, his quick gaze spearing Noah. To the young man his eyes seemed to be as old as the hills. "Don't waste no more of them tears on him. He was a fightin' man. He died fightin'."

With that the wiry little scout was gone in a cloud of dust.

For a long moment Noah stared after the rider while the dust settled around him. Then, reluctantly, he gazed down for the last time at the Apache he had fought, a man no older than Noah himself, a man of pride and strength and courage. A man who would have killed him, Noah thought, but for a chance intervention.

He turned, stumbling, and went in search of his hat. The buckskin stood his ground, waiting until Noah came up to him. Noah stepped into the saddle and groped for the reins. His eyes once more filled with tears.

19

Jessica Allen tumbled out of control down the steep wall of the canyon. Talons of stubby brush clawed at her face and arms and caught her dress, a sharp edge of rock scraped one arm, a flying branch cut her cheek. She was brought up short, the breath knocked out of her, by one hump of rock, but no sooner did she try to grab hold of the surface than she slipped off, fingernails tearing, and fell again. This time she skidded and rolled all the way to the valley floor.

For a moment she lay stunned, her brain whirling, her body so bruised and battered that she could not think.

Had she heard a scream as she fell? Could it have been her own outcry?

Run! she thought. Blaine had been blunt. *When you get to the bottom, run for the station. Don't look back—just run!*

She lay at the base of a manzanita tree, and she used its trunk to brace herself as she struggled to stand. Thinking she heard sounds from far above her on the face of the canyon, she glanced upward but saw nothing. She clambered painfully to her feet, crying out as she put her weight on her left ankle. But it didn't buckle. Somehow she could step on it, gritting her teeth against the pain. Not broken, she thought. A sprain, that's all. He wouldn't even pay attention to such a thing, would he? Or was she foolishly attributing to Cullom Blaine a strength and determination beyond any man?

Jessica hobbled toward the mouth of the canyon. Emerging by the stagecoach road she was surprised at how light it was in the open, how swiftly morning had come.

She glanced anxiously over her shoulder, again searching the east wall of the canyon, which was still deep in shadow. She saw no sign of Blaine. There had been no crack of gunfire or other sounds of battle. Yet she knew that the silence masked a fight to the death.

When Jessica Allen stumbled across the front porch of Cheever's Station and threw herself against the door, she found it barred on the inside. She pounded against the door, sobbing, hysteria threatening to engulf her. "Open up! Please, open the door!"

She didn't hear the bar being lifted. When the door burst open she staggered through the opening.

She found herself staring into the black muzzle of a gun.

"Wait a minute, now. Lemme hear you tell it again." Rimmer lowered the rifle which had confronted her at the door. Jessica recognized it as one of the shining new rifles Rimmer had taken from Cheever's storeroom. Impatiently he waited for her to sit on a nearby bench to relieve the pain of her twisted ankle before he accosted her again. "You're sayin' Blaine told you there was an Injun climbin' down that canyon to get at you?"

"Yes! He heard him!"

"And he told you to light out on your own? To make a run for it?"

"Yes, yes, don't you understand? He wanted me to save myself—to warn all of you!"

Rimmer glanced at the others, who were listening with

varying attitudes of alarm and bewilderment. Jessica saw Charity Calder's eyes fixed on her anxiously. Rimmer's mocking tone drew her attention back to him. "You hear that, folks? Blaine's got our welfare at heart! Kinda turned over a new leaf all of a sudden."

"I'm telling you the truth!" Jessica said hotly, stung by Rimmer's mocking skepticism.

"And you think we should believe you?" Rimmer grinned down at her. "Seems kind of funny he'd keep you with him all last night, and then soon as it was daylight he wanted to get shed of you in a hurry. Jest about the time he figgered someone might come lookin' for him. And I don't mean no Apache."

"That's not the way it was!" Jessica was angry now. "Don't be a fool—there's an Apache out there! And if there's one that means there are more. They haven't left!"

"Now you're an expert on Injuns?" Rimmer scoffed. "You seen this redskin yourself?"

"No—of course not! It was too dark."

"Uh-huh, too dark. But Blaine heard him, that right?"

"Yes! So did I!"

"Apaches is known for that. I mean, bein' heavy-footed like that, so's you always hear 'em comin'."

"Maybe we should listen to her," Art Cheever put in. "If there are Apaches still in the canyon, that means—"

"It means nothin'!" Rimmer snapped. "That's Blaine's story. He knew he couldn't get away if he was saddled with her, so he made up a ghost Indian to scare her and sent her packin'. I'd of done the same, or maybe found another way to keep her quiet." Rimmer's cold grin waited for her to catch his meaning, waited for the horror of it to show in her eyes.

"We can't be sure," the drummer said hesitantly. "If

there's any chance of another attack, we'd better be ready for it."

"My God, aren't any of you listening to me?" Jessica cried. "There's a man out there alone, unarmed—he could be dead by now! Isn't anyone going to do anything to help him?"

Rimmer's reaction was swift. He seized her by the upper arm, his fingers biting cruelly into her flesh. "You sure of that? He don't have no gun?"

"No! He has a knife, that's all. He—" She broke off, realizing too late that she had told Rimmer too much. That her words would not save Cullom Blaine, they condemned him.

"That's all I needed to know!" said Rimmer.

Jessica shrank from the gleam of anticipation in his eyes. What had she done? "I . . . I could be wrong about that . . . about him having a gun. I didn't see one, that's all, but maybe . . ."

Rimmer's grin saw through her feeble pretense. "You two musta got right friendly durin' the night. Since when does a nice soldier's widow take up with an outlaw so quick? Might be that trooper's turnin' over in his grave."

"You've no call to say that!" Clay Adams protested.

Rimmer wheeled on him, and the young stage driver flinched as if shocked by his own daring.

"No?" Rimmer demanded. "You got somethin' to say about it now? You been at that bar whilst I wasn't lookin', swallowin' some courage?"

"I only meant . . . we should listen to what she says . . ."

Adams faltered, his words trailing off. He felt Jessica Allen's gaze upon him and a flush darkened his face. In that instant, as the heat of shame rose in his cheeks, a spark of courage flared where he had thought there was none left. Life wasn't worth living this way, cowering before a bully with a gun, sick with fear and self-loathing. He wouldn't let himself be seen this way!

Stiffening, Clay Adams stuck out his chin in defiance as he confronted Rimmer. "Damn it, I meant what I said. She has no reason to lie. And you have no reason to say other!"

Rimmer acted with brutal swiftness. Taking two quick strides to meet Adams, he swung the barrel of the Colt carbine in a slashing arc. It smacked against the side of Clay Adams' face. The crushing force of the blow knocked the young stage driver off his feet. Blood and bits of broken teeth sprayed from his cut mouth. He lay where he had fallen, only half-conscious as Rimmer swayed over him. For a moment the gunman let the muzzle of the carbine tip toward the fallen man, as if he were about to pull the trigger. Then he stepped back.

"I'll take care of you later!" Rimmer promised harshly. "Right now I got no time. You!" He glared at Cheever. "Watch the doors. Nobody leaves, hear me?"

Cheever's head bobbed eagerly.

"I'm goin' out there to bring Blaine back in. He's cash on the hoof to me, understand? I ain't lettin' him get away."

Rimmer moved quickly to the door and peered out. The rising sun, after its brief moment of glory, chose that moment to dip behind the low cloud layer, and the morning swiftly darkened. Rimmer hesitated a moment before something caught the corner of his eye.

His gaze arrested by a drift of dust about a mile to the east where two riders topped the distant rise, Rimmer failed to glance higher. He did not notice how a sudden gust of wind shredded the message of smoke climbing above the ridgetop against the gray sky.

Cullom Blaine had left his boots behind. He crept on stockinged feet away from the narrow crevice where the woman still lay counting down the minutes. Away from her and away from the Apache who crouched somewhere above him on the canyon wall.

Blaine knew he could not approach the Indian directly or from below. Clambering down to the bottom of the draw seemed to offer little real hope, although there was cover there. The Indian would still be able to sight down on him as soon as it was light enough.

And he would be out of Blaine's reach.

With a gun Blaine's choice might have been different. He had only a knife.

And the element of surprise.

He began to worm his way higher on the face of the canyon, searching out cracks and fissures in the irregular rock where he could grip with hand or foot. He had to test each carefully, first to be sure there was no loose surface to betray him, then to assure himself that the crack or edge of rock would hold his weight. The air was cool but he was soon sweating, and after several minutes the strain was beginning to make itself felt in his hands and arms and legs. He stopped to rest, pressed flat against the slope.

How long now? Concentrating on his climb, he had lost track of the passage of time. Five minutes? Six? He had no way of knowing.

The darkness still pooled in the canyon. He could not make out any clear outlines beyond a few yards. If he couldn't see the Apache, chances were the Apache couldn't see him. But the sky overhead seemed to have lightened even in the brief minutes Blaine had been climbing. Soon the light would begin to penetrate the shadows. It would happen quickly.

When it did Blaine had to be within reach.

The ten minutes were like a noose tightening around his neck. No time to climb higher. He had to gamble that he was now above the Apache.

Blaine began to inch his way to his left, above the niche where Jessica Allen waited, above—Blaine could only hope—the place where the careless young Apache crouched, also waiting.

It happened before Blaine was ready. He was reaching out with his left foot for a narrow step in the rock wall, his full weight borne by his hands and the straining toes of his right foot, a position that left him virtually helpless, when there was a sudden tumult below him.

Good, Jessica! The thought flashed through Blaine's mind with a sting of admiration.

Then, as the thrashing sounds of her fall down the face of the canyon bludgeoned the silence, a dark shape straightened up about fifteen feet below Blaine and almost as far to his left. Close enough for Blaine to see the Apache's arms lift, the barrel of a rifle lancing outward as he took aim.

There wasn't time to think, to weigh the odds, even to measure the distance accurately. The woman had done all he asked, giving him this one moment of surprise, the only one he would have. Blaine pushed himself to his left, recklessly shifted his weight to that foot, twisted his body around and leaped.

It was more free-fall than deliberate jump but it aimed his body like a spear directly at the Apache.

The Indian heard him. He started to turn, whipping the rifle around, but he wasn't quick enough. Blaine smashed into him, head ducked, shoulder driving into the Apache's chest, arms groping wildly.

The force of his dive and the full impact of their collision hurled both men out into space. The Indian's rifle flew from his hands, cartwheeling out of sight into the depths of the canyon.

It was the young Apache's involuntary cry that was heard by Jessica Allen far below—a bleat of terror of the unknown hurtling at him out of the darkness.

The two men crashed onto a narrow ledge too steeply angled to offer much purchase. The Apache's momentary panic vanished as his enemy took human shape and smell and size. Instantly Blaine found himself battling as if he had been dumped inside a barrel with an angry wolf.

They slid along the outcropping, clawing at each other's eyes and faces. Dropping over the edge, they fell together. They bumped down a steep slide, scraped over some sharp-edged corners of rock, and came up short once more, their fall broken by stubby brush.

Blaine drove a fist into the Apache's mouth. The Indian spat blood and struck back. Suddenly a knife appeared in his hand. Blaine caught his wrist in the instant before he could strike. His own knife, sheathed while he had to use both hands during his climb, was at his waist. Blaine groped for it as the thin branches supporting the two men began to bend and break. When he drew the blade he found his own wrist seized at once.

Locked together, neither man able to release his grip on the other's knife arm, Blaine and the Apache broke loose again along the steep slope. Blaine felt the cutting edges of rock and gravel raking his flesh as he rolled and tumbled downward.

He slammed onto his back on another ledge, the young Indian on top of him. The impact exploded the breath from his lungs. Blaine stared into the black eyes of the enemy. For the first time he had the sense of a defined individual as he looked into that dark-skinned, youthful face inches from his own. The bones of the Apache's cheeks and nose and chin were as sharply cut as the knife in his hand. It was a proud, arrogant, even aristocratic face, as well proportioned as his sinewy body. He was neither as tall nor as broad in the chest and shoulders as Blaine, but he was all corded muscle, all hatred, all warrior with blood in his eye.

As they fought, the silence of their struggle broken only by gasps for breath and grunts of effort, neither able to tear his arm free for a knife thrust, Blaine felt himself being forced outward. His head and shoulders projected into space beyond the rocky sill. Sensing advantage, the Apache pressed harder, trying to shove Blaine over the edge. The sharp projection cut into the bow of Blaine's back as the Indian pushed him down with all his strength.

Blaine felt the pull of his own weight now, dragging him downward as most of his body was wrestled off the narrow shelf. His grip on the Apache's wrist began to weaken.

He let go as he went over the edge—but in the moment of feeling the last support disappear under him, leaving only empty space, he grabbed the Apache's ankle and dragged him along.

This time the drop was longer, a plummet into darkness with the slice of morning sky wheeling far above them, like falling into a well. They crashed together into the arms of a big oak and broke apart. Branches slashed across Blaine's face and speared his back. He grunted in pain, unable to breathe. But he lay cradled in the Y of a big branch.

The Apache had fallen away. Blaine heard him spilling down through the branches of the tree. As he struggled for breath and against the darkness that threatened him— somewhere he had taken a blow to the head as he fell— Blaine realized that he had lost his knife. He had no weapons left but courage and the stubborn unwillingness to be beaten.

The thrashing in the branches below him stopped. The canyon was cool and still. Light was beginning to wash down from above, sketching the irregular face of the canyon walls. Blaine twisted his body so that he could peer down into the shadows.

The Apache's uptilted face appeared through the tangle of leaves and branches. He began to climb toward Blaine, slowly, lips bared over his teeth. Blaine felt sympathetic twinges as he made out the bloody lacerations over the Indian's chest and shoulders, the curious way he dragged one leg.

But the Apache kept climbing. As he hauled himself painfully higher, branch by branch, he drew close enough for Blaine to see the sweat on his beardless face, the gleam of the knife blade in his hand. Blaine recognized too the young, untempered warrior's pride that drove the Apache on.

"Let there be no more blood between us," Blaine said quietly. "Go with honor."

Though he spoke in the Apache tongue, the young brave stared up at him as if without comprehension. He caught another branch and gained another foot of the distance between them. He would not quit, Blaine saw. He could not let it go.

He watched the brave's stubborn progress with understanding and acceptance. The man could do no other, not now. He was a fighting man; he was Apache. Blaine could offer him respect. He also meant to offer a proud death.

Out of the corner of his eye Blaine thought he glimpsed a flash of movement down canyon, but he dared not risk a closer look. The Apache was almost within reach now. If others were coming to join him, Blaine would have to face that when it happened. One angry Indian at a time in a tree was enough for any man, he thought.

He let the Apache get close enough to be lured into an attempt at slashing Blaine's foot. At the last moment he drew back out of reach.

The Apache had to lean partly on his free arm for balance, for it was true that one leg had something wrong with it, a twisted knee or broken ankle, forcing him to put all his weight on the good leg. When he hunched himself upward he was momentarily in an awkward position. Blaine grabbed the branch that supported him and swung outward. As the brave twisted to face him Blaine looped around and kicked him in the mouth.

He had aimed for the throat.

The Apache fell out of his perch but other branches caught him, breaking his plunge. He had dropped only six feet or so—and he had hung on to his knife.

While the Indian struggled to right himself, Blaine searched for and broke off a stout branch. The Apache's eyes watched him with hate. There was blood on his cheek and more on his chest where a flap of skin had been peeled back. But he started climbing again, dragging his leg.

Blaine had managed to break off most of the smaller tributary branches as well as the whippy end of the branch before the savage got within reach. He was left with an oaken club nearly the length and thickness of a cane.

The Apache lunged upward with the knife, slashing at the muscles of Blaine's calf, trying to cripple him. Blaine swung his club, missed.

He maneuvered around the thick oak's trunk, forcing the Indian to pull himself after him. Before he was close enough to strike again with the knife, Blaine leaned out and struck with the long branch. It crunched solidly against the man's collarbone.

The blow must have paralyzed the Apache's arm for a moment. The knife fell away from nerveless fingers to vanish among the leaves and branches below. With a yell of rage he hurled himself recklessly upward. He grabbed the end of Blaine's staff, the movement so swift that Blaine was jerked off balance before he could let go. His foot slipped from the branch where he had braced himself. He spun off his perch and tumbled into the Apache.

They fell together through the tree toward the ground, locked in a deathly embrace, spilling from branch to branch. And at the last there was a free-fall, an unbroken drop of about ten feet through an opening.

By chance alone Blaine was on top during that last twisting plunge. The Apache struck the ground first with his head and shoulders taking the full weight of impact, his own and Blaine's. There was a crack of bone snapping, not unlike the sound when Blaine had broken off the branch. The Apache's head was bent at an odd angle.

Blaine rolled off him.

He lay still for a long minute, unable to move, struggling even to breathe. Then, as he turned to look amid the leaves and debris on the canyon floor for the Apache's dropped knife and rifle, Blaine saw someone step into view on a ledge about fifteen feet above him.

He stared down the gleaming barrel of the Colt carbine in Rimmer's hands, the shiny new weapon with the revolving cylinder that Rimmer had taken from Cheever's storeroom. Blaine followed the brush stroke of light along the barrel to the glitter of amusement in Rimmer's eyes.

"Judas Priest, I never thought you could whip him," Rimmer said with a chuckle. "Hell of a fight, I almost hated to see it end." He paused a moment, as if assaying the bloody, battered figures on the ground beneath him, the live one hardly in better condition than the dead man. "Too bad, Blaine. I can't risk takin' you back alive. You're too tricky by half. Them Clancy boys is comin' down the road. Should be there at the station when I drag you in, but I reckon they will just have to pay up for the carcass." He grinned again. "Say your prayers, Blaine, you've kilt your last Injun . . ."

Blaine stared up at him, helpless, unable to evade the bullet that would smash into him as Rimmer slowly squeezed the trigger.

Blaine was left stunned, ears humming, his face cut by flying bits of metal as the carbine blew up in Rimmer's face.

20

Tom and Art Clancy came on the run, riding hell for leather down the long grade from the east toward Cheever's Station, Tom spooked by the possibility of confronting Apaches, but there were none in sight. The station caught a little spear of sunlight for a moment before clouds shut it off. The smoke seen earlier above the hills was no longer visible; there was only a curl of smoke from a chimney at the back of the station. Maybe that was what we saw, Tom hoped, no doubt a cooking fire, nothing threatening about it.

As the riders swept in, a few people came out onto the long veranda in front of the station, tentatively at first, as if uncertain whether the hoofbeats portended good or bad. Several of them seemed more interested in the canyon on the north side of the trail than in the newcomers. Cheever, the station owner, was one of these. He looked kind of sickly, Art Clancy thought, as if he had swallowed something he didn't like.

The Clancy brothers hauled up in front of the station, dust skidding on ahead of them, and at that moment, just when Tom had his mouth open to speak—Tom could never wait to get in the first word, even with strangers—there was the crash of a gun from somewhere in the canyon, only the single report, very loud, reminding Art more of a small cannon than a rifle or six-shooter. The brothers exchanged startled glances.

Rimmer was not among those on the porch.

"What the hell was that?" Tom Clancy asked. He had the look in his eyes that Art didn't like, the rolling-eyed look of a buffalo seeing the hunter.

"Take it easy," Art snapped. "You don't see these womenfolk throwin' a fit, do you?"

The scornful remark was meant to shake Tom up, quell that sudden mindless panic that could make him do or say something foolish. It had the desired effect as Tom took in the group on the porch, who seemed disturbed by the explosion in the canyon but not unduly alarmed.

"You'd best come inside," Cheever said. He didn't look much happier than Tom did. "Ain't none of us doin' any good out here on the porch." His gaze roved uneasily over the surrounding hills. *He's scared*, Art Clancy saw, and he thought immediately of the smoking hills.

The Clancy brothers turned their horses into the corral and hurried inside the station. There were women as well as men inside, a fact explained by the stagecoach resting at the side of the station. But where were their horses?

Excited voices began to answer the questions. It took a minute or two before Art sorted out what was being said so that he could put the facts together. Cheever's Station had been hit by Apaches, who had stolen horses from the corral and fired on the station. The Indians had withdrawn at dusk the previous day after the fighting had dwindled to an occasional rifle shot. Several of the men said the raids were over, a drummer most insistently. There was, Art thought, a quality of wishful thinking in his insistence.

The news about Apaches sent Tom Clancy to the bar at the back of the room for a glass of whiskey. But he was quick to pick up on the hopeful words of the drummer. Hell, it hadn't been much of a raid at all. And it was over.

What interested Tom Clancy then was the news about Rimmer and Cullom Blaine. Both had been at the station. The surprise was that Blaine had been a prisoner of Marshal J. P. Holifield. Where was Holifield? To the brothers' astonishment they learned—the talkative drummer was firm about it—that Blaine had gunned down the marshal. Rimmer had caught him in the act, put him down and tied him up.

"Damn all, we shoulda been here to see that!" Tom exclaimed. "Wouldn't you like to seen that, Art?"

But the night before, in the aftermath of the Indian raid, Blaine had escaped. There was some confusion about how it had happened. One woman tried to defend Blaine —it seemed that Blaine had taken her with him when he escaped but later released her. She tried to say something about Apaches but the others interrupted. Rimmer, they said, had gone into the canyon after Blaine only a few minutes before the Clancy brothers pulled up before the station. There'd been no sound until the single explosion everyone had heard.

"Rimmer got him!" Tom said excitedly to his brother. "Now we'll have to pay up." He sounded momentarily aggrieved. "Hell, I wanted to do it myself."

Art Clancy let it go. Sometimes it did Tom good to bluster a little.

As the realization took hold that Cullom Blaine was cut down at last, no longer a dark shadow waiting around every corner for him, Tom Clancy began to experience a state of euphoria. "Hallelujah!" he whooped, clapping his brother on the back, sending up a small cloud of dust from his shirt. "This is our day to celebrate!"

"You won't be celebrating if the Apaches hit us again," the woman said caustically, the one who had tried to defend Cullom Blaine against criticism.

For her part Jessica Allen was horrified by everything she saw in the two men lately arrived. These were two of the men Blaine hunted! Rough, callous, bullying outlaws, as bad as Rimmer or worse. She thought of Samantha Blaine attacked in her own house by a pack of such men, and shuddered . . .

"Ain't no Apaches," Tom Clancy said with a grin. "We'd of seen 'em when we come in if'n they was there. You think they'd of let us ride in whole like that?"

He went to the front door and stepped out onto the long veranda. "Hey, Rimmer!" he shouted, cupping his hands around his mouth.

"Hold on a minute, Tom!" his brother cautioned. "Let's make sure we know the bull's been dehorned before you grab hold."

But Tom Clancy, his elation and relief over Blaine's undoing making him reckless enough to defy his smarter brother, shook off the warning and stepped down from the porch. "Rimmer!" he called again. "This here's Tom Clancy! Where's your prize bull—"

No one knew exactly what he had meant to say. The yell choked off. An arrow jutted from his throat.

His breathing cut off, Tom clawed at the terrifying obstruction with both hands, for some seconds not knowing what it was, what had happened to him. He heard the crackle of gunfire then, and through it a rush of shrill, blood-chilling screeches. Oh my God, war cries!

Falling to his knees, he saw the Apaches erupt from the grass and the hollows and the river bottom all around Cheever's Station.

The growth along the canyon bottom was thick with wild flowers, luxuriant grasses and a variety of trees—the big oak in which Blaine and the Apache had fought, along with black walnut, ash and juniper trees. Near where Blaine lay, a morning flower, pale blue in color, peeped among a tangle of vines and fallen limbs.

And in the silence that followed the explosion of Cheever's Colt carbine in Rimmer's hands, life began to stir in the canyon. A squirrel popped over a tumble of rocks, halted to stare nervously at Blaine, then scurried away as Blaine struggled to rise. A moment later Blaine heard a rustle among some leaves and caught a glimpse of a deer bounding lightly away, tail bobbing for a moment before it vanished into the depths of the canyon.

What the awakening told Blaine was that he had no other enemies in the immediate vicinity. An Apache might hide from a man, but not from the alert animal life of the wilderness.

He found that he could move his limbs, and once he was on his feet the dizziness—aftermath of a blow he had taken to the head—began to ebb. Slowly, testing himself, he circled the base of the big oak. He moved out in widening circles, scanning the thick undergrowth for a gleam of metal.

The Apache's rifle had flown much farther out than Blaine had anticipated, but at last he saw the barrel poking at him from between two rocks. It gave him a start, the barrel aimed at Blaine's chest almost as if an unseen rifleman held it there. But the position was an accident of the weapon's fall.

Blaine saw with relief that the gun seemed undamaged. It was a scarred but serviceable Spencer. It was a repeater but not one of Cheever's fancy guns, Blaine thought, remembering the station owner's unease and his silence.

A thought came unbidden. *He knew. Knew it would blow up in Rimmer's face if he tried to fire it, and let it*

happen. Knew—and here Blaine could only surmise—
because it had happened before.

Blaine had heard stories about the Colt revolving-cylinder carbine, recounting its unfortunate tendency sometimes to fire all chambers simultaneously instead of the
one where the hammer struck. The mishaps explained
why a weapon with such a familiar and seemingly useful
design had never won favor on the frontier when compared with the more conventional but reliable old Sharps
and Henry and Spencer rifles, or the newer Winchesters.

And might a bad batch of rifles explain Cheever's fear of
Navaja? His gloomy certainty that Navaja had come for
more than horses? An Apache bent on vengeance would
let nothing stop him, especially if it was personal.

And here Blaine thought suddenly of the rumored
death of Navaja's brother in last winter's skirmishing with
the cavalry. If Cheever had sold some of those Colts to
Navaja and his renegades, that would explain a lot of
things. It would explain why the remaining weapons in
the box, all spanking new, had never been sold or fired. It
would explain Cheever's silence in the face of Rimmer's
bullying. It might even explain why the Apaches were
short of firepower, as evidenced by the scarcity of shooting through most of the previous afternoon. The Indians
wouldn't trust any of the Colt weapons they had purchased if even one of them had blown up in some unlucky
brave's hands. It would explain most of all why Navaja had
called his followers together for a reckless raid on
Cheever's Station, persisted in even after the successful
theft of the horses. It would explain the smoking hills.

Examining the recovered Spencer, Blaine found that it
held two of its copper-cased cartridges in the magazine
and another in the chamber. Three shots in all.

His memory locked on what Rimmer had said: *Them*

*Clancy boys is comin' down the road, should be there at
the station when I drag you in . . .*

Three bullets, Blaine thought grimly. Three would be
enough for the Clancy brothers. There were but two of
them.

He started toward the mouth of the canyon, watching
the cliffs as well as the canyon floor. Navaja had left a
sentry posted up on the cliffs for a reason. He would be
back. If Blaine was right in his hunch, the Apache was on a
mission of vengeance that would not end while Cheever
was alive.

Near the mouth of the canyon a tumble of rocks forced
Blaine toward the stream. He flattened himself on the
ground and wormed his way around the rocks, not trusting the streambed which less than twenty-four hours ago
had swarmed with redskins. He was not yet in sight of
Cheever's Station when he heard someone shouting.
"Rimmer!"

Blaine recognized the voice almost instantly. A surge of
rage nearly drove him to his feet in reckless disregard of
danger. He sank back, instinct warning him he was not
alone.

"Rimmer! This here's Tom Clancy! Where's your
prize . . ."

Blaine didn't hear the rest of it. He had seen a painted
face peering over the edge of a hollow off to the left of
Cheever's Station. Almost immediately bodies erupted
from the surrounding brush and grasses, and the shrill
terror of the Apache attack broke against the beleaguered
station. Cullom Blaine knew then that he had miscalcu-
lated . . . that three bullets might have been enough to
take him against the Clancy brothers but left him badly
shortchanged for what now lay ahead. Trapped at the
mouth of the canyon, away from the protection of the

station, the moment he made any kind of move at all he would be surrounded by Navaja and his renegades.

Still far to the south, Lieutenant Arnold Wilson rode at full gallop at the front of his detachment of troops. He knew he would have to call a breather soon, that the horses would have to be rested if ónly briefly. The men themselves, after a tedious and mostly boring mission, were all too eager for battle, ready to push on if he gave the order.

Glancing over his shoulder, Wilson saw the young Shaker lad's coat billowing out behind him like a giant cape as he rode. Courageous thing to do, Wilson acknowledged, sneaking through the Apache lines alone and riding for help. But the young man had been regrettably vague about the things Wilson needed to know—the number of Apaches most particularly. He had spoken of "a horde" and "great numbers" of Indians all around Cheever's Station. But how dependable could the observations of an excited Easterner be?

For better or worse, Arnold Wilson had made his decision. He was risking his detachment—and his career—if he encountered Navaja and an overwhelming force of Apaches. His judgment and limited experience in the field argued that Navaja's war party would be relatively small. Even if it numbered as many as forty or fifty braves —and Wilson did not believe this probable—the well-rested, well-armed fighting men of the cavalry ought to be able to handle them.

Unless they blundered into a trap.

If the Shaker youth's report was accurate, Navaja would not be expecting the detachment to return—might even have counted on the fact that it was heading back to Fort Tracy. In that event Wilson, not Navaja, would be the one to spring a surprise. The possibility fanned the excitement in the officer's breast.

With an effort of will Lieutenant Wilson threw up his hand and called a halt to the cavalry's punishing ride. As the troopers milled around him, reluctant to stop, Wilson called out above the familiar jingle of gear and the stamping of hoofs. "Ten minutes! No more! Rest and check your gear. Then let's go catch some Apaches!"

21

Within Cheever's Station panic flew like fear through a chicken coop.

Art Clancy ran to the door. He took one look at his brother Tom sinking to his knees, clawing at the arrow that stuck out from his throat, and a bellow of rage shook him. "Goddam you, Tom, I tol' you! You never listen!"

A bullet thudded into the door frame inches from Art's head. He jerked back instinctively into the station and hauled the door shut. Without thinking he dropped the bar into place.

He had always helped Tom, always steered him shy of trouble when he could. He could not help Tom now.

His bitter rage condensed into tears. This was all Cullom Blaine's doing! He regretted in that instant that Rimmer had already shot Blaine. Or so he'd been led to believe.

It flicked through his mind that Rimmer had been trapped in the canyon. Even if Blaine had managed to turn the tables on him, which hardly seemed possible, the survivor was at the mercy of Navaja and his Apaches. The bounty hunter would never collect his fee. Tom would have been glad.

Cheever was shouting angrily. Art Clancy took in the pandemonium inside the station—a dumpy woman sobbing beside a cot on which a man lay with his neck swathed in bandages, the dude with the look of a drummer wringing his hands while Cheever yelled at him and shoved a rifle toward him, a muscular waddy with a puffed-up mouth and a dazed look about his eyes stumbling toward one of the loopholes with his gun, a white-faced girl in a plain dress and prim little bonnet sitting quietly on a bench as if removed from the turmoil all about her, another woman purposefully shouldering a rifle at one of the slits in the west wall and squeezing off a shot.

A chill crept along Clancy's spine. The ragtag lot in Cheever's Station could not hold out for long against the fury of the Apache attack. Some of the Indians had reached the veranda. Art could hear them out there—a tomahawk smashing against the door, a thumping overhead as one of the savages vaulted onto the roof, a shrieking of war cries . . .

Suddenly a rifle barrel jabbed through a loophole from the outside. Art stepped toward it swiftly as flame spurted from the muzzle. Drawing his six-gun with practiced skill, he shoved it to the opening and squeezed off a blind shot. He heard the Apache on the veranda cry out.

Something crashed against the front door. Something heavy, solid, shaking the door on its hinges, making the whole building shudder. The chill of fear reached Art Clancy's brain. They were smashing down the door! He had to get out!

He had no thought of the others within the station, or of his brother lying wounded or dead in the dust outside. He had to get out—to save himself!

Clancy ran toward the back of the station where he had seen a portion of the kitchen through the open door. Someone got in his way. He shouldered past, sending a figure flying. He stumbled into the kitchen with its wood smoke and coffee smells, saw another door and lunged toward it.

The door smashed inward. By luck Art Clancy was behind it as a painted, red-skinned warrior burst through the opening. The Apache, taller and more physically imposing than most, was so lethal a figure in that tiny room that Art Clancy stood frozen in terror. But the Indian did not see him. He leaped toward the main room of the station.

Clancy spilled outside through the open doorway.

He ran, awkward in his high-heeled boots but with fear shooting through his system to lend him wings. He saw one Indian off to the side and snapped a shot at him. The brave went down.

The corral loomed ahead. Relief made Clancy stumble, his heart lurching in his chest. He could not believe his luck! His own and Tom's horses still stood in the corral. In their haste the brothers had not even stripped the saddles from their mounts before hurrying into the station. Art knew if he reached his horse he had a chance. Indians were poor shots at best and it was always hard to hit a running target.

Reaching the pole gate of the corral, Art Clancy threw it open and ran toward his horse. He was grasping for the reins when out of the corner of his eye he saw another figure rise from the brush at the edge of the stream that ran below the corral. Art ducked instinctively. He turned in a crouch toward the new danger, six-gun level in his hand.

He recognized Cullom Blaine.

Blaine had been puzzled by the direction and fury of the Apaches' frontal assault against Cheever's Station. But the attack was hardly under way before he realized that there were few if any Indians remaining along the riverbed west and south of the station.

The tactic was unusual for any Indian raid but Blaine didn't pause to figure it out. He jumped at the opening offered him.

Scuttling to his right, Blaine found no redskins before him. Worming through tall grass he reached the edge of the stage road. Now he could see the veranda across the front of the station—and a half-dozen Apaches running toward the steps, driving a thick log toward the door!

More Apaches swarmed around the front of the building, ducking below the firing ports. The puzzle of their tactics lingered in Blaine's mind, but he took advantage of the shock of the first impact when the battering ram crashed against the door. Jumping to his feet, he ran across the road.

Dropping low again, Blaine kept to the cover of grass and, nearer the stream, the screen of brush and cottonwoods along its bank. No Apaches rose from the grass or stepped from behind a tree to face him. Their onslaught continued unabated against the front of the station.

Blaine intended to work along the bank past the corral until he could use the stables as cover to get closer to the main building. At one point where thick brush barred his way, he ducked below the bank and trotted along the edge of the stream.

When he found a clearing and raised his head, he saw Art Clancy.

By then Clancy was halfway to the corral. It was plain what he was after—the two horses in the corral still wore their saddles. Blaine climbed up the bank, carrying the scarred old Spencer rifle he had claimed from the dead Apache.

He called out but Art Clancy didn't hear him. Art

grabbed for the reins of the nearest horse as Blaine stepped into the open. Art must have seen him then because he spun in a crouch, six-gun in his hand.

Inside Cheever's Station Navaja struck swiftly. All eyes were on the front door where savages ran a ten-foot ram, hacked from a fallen tree, at the thick wood planks of the door. All except those of Woman, who flew at him with a knife in her hand.

Navaja sidestepped. His own blade swiped across her throat.

As she fell away the Apache chief glided through the kitchen doorway into the main room of the station. His hard black gaze speared Cheever in an instant, and hatred for his enemy filled the warrior's heart.

Cheever sensed him coming. He had been diverted like the others by the attack at the front door—just as Navaja had planned it—and he did not react to the real threat until Navaja was halfway across the room.

He spun around, his face the one the Apache remembered, the face Navaja had kept before him through the long winter, with its watery eyes and lying mouth. He tried to bring his rifle around in time but Navaja was upon him like a big cat, striking with his knife. Blood spurted from Cheever's arm over the stock of his rifle. The gun slipped from his hands.

Others were aware of Navaja by this time, but the Apache stepped behind Cheever and locked an arm around his neck. He wrestled the struggling white man across the room toward the back door, keeping Cheever's body between him and the people in the station. Bleats of terror broke from Cheever's throat. The others could not fire without fear of hitting him.

Navaja reached the kitchen doorway and backed through, dragging Cheever along.

Woman threw herself on his back, slashing with her knife.

Though wounded in this renewed assault, Navaja shrugged her off as if she'd been a blanket. Weak from her own deep cut, she fell in a heap. Her feeble attack had been a final desperate attempt to save or avenge her man.

Navaja gave her no further thought. He backed out of the station into the open. There Cheever made his last-ditch bid to escape. When the brightness of daylight spilled over him he knew himself truly lost. With the strength of the damned he broke Navaja's grip on his neck and stumbled free.

Navaja caught him at the door. "My brother's spirit lives in my hand!" he cried aloud.

His knife flashed in two swift strokes, back and forth, almost severing Cheever's head from his body.

The warrior knelt beside his fallen enemy and the knife flashed again, claiming his trophy, the long-fringed scalp that would hang forever on his lance, a trophy of war through which his brother's spirit would find peace.

Then Navaja was on his feet, running toward the line of cottonwoods along the stream behind the station.

From the firing port in the west wall of the station Jessica Allen saw Art Clancy running toward the corral. She watched him with a flare of contempt. To her own horror she had to resist the temptation to train her sights on his fleeing back. Was it because he was abandoning everyone else to save his own skin? Or because he was responsible for Cullom Blaine's death?

Not knowing the answer, she watched him go.

Fresh turmoil broke out in the station, drawing Jessica

away from the loophole an instant before Blaine stepped into view. Through stunned eyes she saw a fierce Apache leap upon Cheever. Where had he come from? How had he got inside? A heavy knife blade seemed part of his hand, red with blood. Others cried out, and Jessica frantically surveyed the room, half expecting to see more savages spilling through the doors.

But there was only the one. He backed away, holding Art Cheever before him, one arm around Cheever's neck and the other brandishing his knife. Everyone stood helpless. Jessica stared in awe at the fierce proud visage of the Indian glaring at her over Cheever's shoulder.

Then he was through the door, backing into the kitchen and out of sight. She could not see what happened next, but she heard Cheever cry out . . .

And abruptly there was silence.

No one moved. The guns were silent. It was a long moment before Jessica Allen realized that the silence was pervasive. The people inside had ceased firing; the guns outside were also stilled. The shuddering blows against the door from the veranda had ceased.

In the stillness Mildred Sanderson's low moan was like a scream.

A shot drew Jessica back to the loophole behind her. This time she saw Cullom Blaine and Art Clancy framed in the opening, and her knees gave way.

Art Clancy had the advantage, with a six-gun in his practiced hand and the distance between him and Blaine no more than forty feet.

But Blaine appeared before him like an apparition, and the shock of recognition sent a tremor down Art's arm and into his gun hand as he fired.

Art's bullet slapped the trunk of a cottonwood behind

Blaine as the hasty shot missed. Blaine held a rifle in both hands, and he fired from the hip, shooting without aiming the way a gunfighter handled a six-gun.

Art felt the hot lead smash into his chest, driving him back. Damn Blaine anyway, he was a ghost, he couldn't still be alive!

Art Clancy's well-notched revolver kicked once more in his hand, but by then the barrel had tilted downward and his last shot plowed up dust.

Coldly, feeling neither remorse nor satisfaction, Cullom Blaine turned away from Art Clancy's body in the dust of the corral. He knew he had only two bullets left in the Spencer when he saw an Apache crouched over another lifeless heap near the back door to Cheever's Station. The warrior rose in one swift motion and ran toward the stream. He stopped in his tracks when he saw Blaine facing him.

Blaine knew at once that this was Navaja. There was a fierce pride in the warrior's bearing, the arrogance of a chief in the black eyes that glared at Blaine. And when he saw the bloody scalp the warrior carried in one hand Blaine suddenly understood why the Apaches had struck with such noisy fury at the front of the station. They had drawn the defenders toward the front while Navaja slipped in the back way to find Cheever.

Navaja carried no rifle, only his scalp trophy and a bloody knife.

The two men faced each other, each in a fighting crouch, twenty feet apart.

Navaja's head jerked up. Blaine heard it too—the stirring call of a bugle!

Navaja's hot eyes met Blaine's again, then dropped toward the muzzle of the Spencer rifle that was centered on his chest. Blaine tilted the barrel to the side.

Without a word or a sign the Apache chief leaped in catlike bounds toward the stream, vanished down its bank and was gone.

When the cavalry charge spilled around Cheever's Station, there was not an Apache in sight.

22

What a strange man! From the shade of the veranda Jessica Allen watched Cullom Blaine limp across the wagon road, returning from the canyon. He had seemed more preoccupied with retrieving his boots from the ledge where he had left them than with the events swirling around him.

Wearing his boots, Blaine trudged up the steps to the long porch, paused as his gaze settled on her, and then joined her at the rail. After a moment's silence she asked, "Will the cavalry catch any of them?"

The young officer at the head of the detachment had been red-faced with angry disappointment to find all of the Apaches vanished into the hills. The lieutenant had led his troops in pursuit to the west where the largest number of the Indians seemed to have fled. That was nearly an hour ago, and those left behind at Cheever's Station had heard nothing of the outcome.

"A few stragglers maybe. I don't think Navaja wanted a fight with the cavalry, leastwise not just yet."

After a moment's silence she said, "I saw what happened out back. You are no murderer."

"I do what I have to do."

"Yes . . . but no more than that."

Blaine met her gaze stonily. How easy to misunderstand that look! He said, "Art Clancy was one of the men who . . ."

"I know," Jessica said. "And he would have killed you. He and his brother . . . they sent that gunman after you."

Blaine shrugged. "He wasn't much of a gunman."

The silence lengthened between them. She was not sure what the continued silence meant, the reluctance she felt in Blaine to end this moment of isolation together on the veranda, but wings of hope began to flutter in her chest. "You might have killed that Apache," she said at last. "Why didn't you?"

"He wasn't my enemy," Blaine answered quietly. "He was Cheever's. And there was nothing I could do for Cheever."

She nodded, though she did not completely understand. Navaja had come after Cheever, that much was clear. Was that all he was after? Did so many have to suffer for the enmity of one man for another?

"A killer," she said, "would not put so fine a point on it. Especially regarding the life of a savage."

"Navaja will not be free long," Blaine said. "The cavalry will catch up with him sooner or later. Or he'll decide to come in to the reservation again. His time is short."

As if to rebut his comment a group of riders appeared over the low rise west of the station, following the stage-coach road. They wore the blue of cavalrymen, and they walked their horses, the excitement of the chase over. There were no prisoners among them.

Jessica Allen thought of Joe. She guessed that she would never see a cavalry uniform again without thinking of him with a tug of sadness.

"And what of the men you hunt, Mr. Blaine?" She risked the question, her heart pounding. "Are there still others like the Clancy brothers that you must find?"

He was silent for so long that she thought he would

refuse to answer her. Finally, not looking at her but gazing far off at some distant vision, Blaine said, "I have some land I haven't seen for a long time. It is over near Martinsville. I thought I might ride that way." There was a grave he had not visited in too long, he thought. And smaller graves beside it.

"I see," Jessica said, though she was not sure she did. She felt unaccountably close to tears.

Cullom Blaine turned to stare at her then, and in the brightness of the morning even on the shaded veranda she saw that his eyes had flecks of green in them. He said, "If you like Texas at all, Mrs. Allen, I'm sure you'd like it there . . . if you were ever to come that way."

"I'm sure I . . ." She hesitated, frightened. Then with a deep sigh, feeling for all the world like someone flinging herself off a cliff, she said, "I'm sure I will."

The young couple sitting close together on the long bench in a corner of Cheever's Station had eyes only for each other. Charity Calder touched her handkerchief gently to the corner of Noah's swollen mouth, causing him to wince. "It's as well I did not see thee fight," she said. "I do not know what I would have done."

"Does thee blame me?"

Slowly she shook her head. "I am proud of thee, Noah. And I do not think I care if anyone sees me sitting so close to thee," she said.

Noah put an arm around her shoulders, drew her close, and managed a grin. "Nor do I," he said.

They were of the world now, and of its people.